"You've seen *what I can do, Mike,"* Gillian said. *"You know I don't lose my cool when things go boom."*

"Maybe not on the firing range or at a trap shoot, Gillian. They're a world away from the streets and sewers that spawn the kind of garbage we run up against." His eyes never left hers. "The same streets and sewers spawned me. When I fight, I fight dirty. In ways a girl with a lifetime membership to the Rocks Springs Golf and Country Club would never stomach."

"So that's it." Uncurling, she snapped her champagne glass down on the coffee table. It was time…*past* time…that Hawk opened his eyes and saw her as she was, not as he wanted to see her.

"First," she said, "I stopped being a girl years ago. Second, I can handle whatever crawls out of a sewer. And that—" she stabbed her forefinger into his chest "—includes you, Michael Callahan."

Bunching her fists into his shirt, she swooped in. The heat, the anger fused her lips to his. When he remained rigid and unresponsive, sheer stubbornness took over. She altered her angle of attack and covered her mouth over his.

Dear Reader,

I first visited Hong Kong on my honeymoon. I was a young lieutenant stationed in Taiwan at the time and absolutely fell in love with the fabled city that combined British ambiance with a Chinese history that went back for millennia. I remember thinking then that the broad boulevards and narrow, teeming alleys made the perfect setting for a novel.

I didn't follow up on that thought until my husband and I went back to Hong Kong last year for a brief visit. Once again, the exotic mix of cultures captured my heart and my imagination.

So I hope you enjoy this tale of danger, intrigue and sizzling romance set against the backdrop of one of the world's most dazzling cities.

Merline Lovelace

MERLINE LOVELACE

Undercover Wife

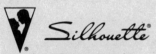

Romantic

SUSPENSE

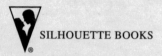 **SILHOUETTE BOOKS**

ISBN-13: 978-0-373-27601-1
ISBN-10:   0-373-27601-X

UNDERCOVER WIFE

Printed in U.S.A.

Books by Merline Lovelace

Silhouette Romantic Suspense

*Code Name: Danger
†Men of the Bar H
‡To Protect and Defend

MERLINE LOVELACE

A retired U.S. Air Force colonel, Merline Lovelace served at bases all over the world, including Taiwan, Vietnam and at the Pentagon. When she hung up her uniform for the last time, she decided to combine her love of adventure with a flair for storytelling, basing many of her tales on her experiences in the service.

Since then, she's produced more than seventy action-packed novels, many of which have been on the *USA TODAY* and Waldenbooks bestseller lists. Over nine million copies of her works are in print in thirty-one countries. Named Oklahoma's Writer of the Year and the Oklahoma Female Veteran of the Year, Merline is also a recipient of the Romance Writers of America's prestigious RITA® Award.

When she's not glued to her keyboard, she and her husband enjoy traveling and chasing little white balls around the fairways of Oklahoma. Check her Web site at www.merlinelovelace.com for news, contests and information about upcoming releases.

To my handsome husband and those magical days and nights in Hong Kong. Who wudda thunk the honeymoon would last for thirty-eight years and counting.

Prologue

"What do you think it is?"

His voice muffled by his surgical mask, the pathologist at the U.S. Fish and Wildlife Service Forensics Lab yielded his place at the electron microscope to his partner.

"Damned if I know," the second scientist answered as he peered at the sample taken from the carcass. "It doesn't match any known viral strains."

He straightened, and both men's glances went to the glass enclosure separating them from the creature stretched out on the autopsy table. It was a *nomascus concolor,* or Western black-crested gibbon, very rare and native to the jungles of Asia. The two pathologists had no idea how it had made its way to the ditch beside California's Highway 101 where it had been found dead, its carcass pecked almost to pieces by crows. The fact that those same crows lay in lifeless heaps beside the gibbon raised an immediate red flag with the road worker who stumbled across them. Within hours, local authorities, worried about a possible outbreak of avian flu, had sealed and shipped the remains to the U.S. Fish and Wildlife Service Forensics Lab in Oregon.

The pathologists performing the autopsy could confirm that bird flu had killed neither the monkey nor the crows. The mounting evidence of what *had* killed them scared the crap out of both scientists.

"Looks like we've got us a mutant virus," the senior member of the team acknowledged reluctantly. "Very contagious and very deadly. We need to issue an immediate alert."

The alert went out to all government agencies. The Centers for Disease Control reissued it to the civilian sector, where everyone not directly involved in health care or simian research pretty much ignored it.

Except for one individual halfway around the world. When the alert painted across the screen of a computer configured to search for such items, it was read with fierce, almost primal satisfaction.

"Soon." Exultation shattered the stillness of the darkened room. "Soon my revenge will be complete."

Chapter 1

The town house halfway down a side street just off Massachusetts Avenue, in the heart of Washington, D.C.'s embassy district, looked much like its neighbors. It boasted an elegant, federal-style facade and tall windows framed by black shutters. A short flight of steps led to an oak door painted in gleaming vermilion.

A bronze plaque beside the door identified the town house as home to the offices of the president's Special Envoy. The position was one of those jobs created to reward rich campaign contributors with a yen for a Washington office and a taste of power politics. Only a handful of insiders knew the Special Envoy also served as Director of OMEGA, a supersecret government agency with an elite cadre of operatives activated only in extreme emergencies.

It wasn't an emergency that had brought a small legion of agents in from the various ventures that provided cover in their civilian lives, however. They were gathered in the director's office to welcome back one of their own.

Elizabeth Wells had served as executive assistant to OMEGA's director for almost two decades. The silver-haired grandmother had fallen while doing a foxtrot on a big-band cruise of the Potomac with her latest beau. After hip-replacement surgery and months of rehab, Elizabeth was ready to resume her duties.

Three of her bosses were present for the homecoming. Adam Ridgeway, code name Thunder, had hired Elizabeth all those years ago. Tall and broad-shouldered, Thunder stood with one hand in the pocket of his hand-tailored slacks and a pained expression on his face while his wife—also a former operative and one-time OMEGA director—related the latest exploits of their youngest.

"Tank insists it wasn't his idea." With a rueful grin, Maggie Sinclair, code name Chameleon, continued her description of her son's assault on the hallowed halls of Harvard. "He also insists he did *not* position Terence atop the bust of John Adams, at the perfect angle to spit into the face of the dean of the Business School."

Terence, as the assembled operatives all knew, was the orange-and-purple-striped iguana Maggie had brought back from a mission in Central America years ago. The evil-tempered creature was the bane of Adam's existence. He'd been looking forward to its demise for as long as anyone could remember, but his wife and three children adored the damned thing. So much so that

Adam Jr.—known to his family and friends as Tank—
had carted off the lizard with him to enjoy the delights
of his freshman year at Harvard.

Tank's sister took up the tale at that point. "You
should have seen Dad's face when the dean called."

Laughter sparkled in Gillian Ridgeway's vivid blue
eyes. She had her father's gleaming black hair and aristocratic features. From her mother, she'd inherited a flair
for languages and an irrepressible sense of humor. On
extended leave from her job with the State Department,
Gillian had filled in as executive assistant to OMEGA's
director during Elizabeth Wells's convalescence.

"Dad won't say what it cost to keep both Tank and
Terence on the student rolls, but I suspect Harvard got
a hefty endowment out of it."

"I suspect they'll get *several* endowments before
Tank graduates."

That came from Nick Jensen, code name Lightning,
OMEGA's current director. Lightning had headed the
agency through three successive presidential adminis-
trations. Although he hadn't made a formal announcement, the betting was he'd resign the directorship after
the upcoming election. When his wife, Mackenzie, surprised herself and everyone else by turning up pregnant
with their first child, the bet had become a sure thing.

"There she is!"

Alerted by a glimpse through the window of a sleek
limo gliding to a halt at the curb, Lightning strode out
to greet his executive assistant. A few moments later
he escorted the slender, gray-haired grandmother into
his office.

Agents with code names such as Slash, Rogue, Cowboy, Diamond and Cyrene welcomed her with warm hugs. Elizabeth had tears in her eyes when Maggie gave her shoulders a gentle squeeze and Adam dropped an affectionate kiss on her cheek. While the champagne corks popped, Elizabeth dabbed her eyes with a lace-trimmed handkerchief before proceeding to stun the entire gathering.

"I have an announcement. I'm afraid my return is only temporary."

Instant concern replaced the smiles and good wishes. Lightning's voice went taut. "What's happened? Did you experience complications you didn't tell me about during my last visit?"

"As a matter of fact, I did." Her pale blue eyes filled with a combination of chagrin and delight. "I'm getting married next month. Next week, if Daniel has his way."

After a few seconds of stunned silence, Lightning recovered. "Daniel? Who the hell is this character, and why didn't you let us check him out?"

"You did. Very thoroughly, as I recall. It's Daniel Foster. *Dr.* Daniel Foster."

"Your surgeon?"

"One and the same." A hint of red crept into Elizabeth's cheeks. "Apparently he thinks I have rather elegant hips, before and after the surgery. *I* think he just wants to admire his handiwork."

Whoops erupted throughout the room. When they subsided and champagne flutes made their way into everyone's hands, Lightning lifted his glass.

"To you and Dr. Dan. He'd better make you *very*

happy or some extremely lethal undercover agents will show up on his doorstep."

Several similar toasts later, Elizabeth brought up the subject of her successor. Her expression was as warm as her voice when she turned to Gillian.

"Lightning says you did a magnificent job covering for me, Jilly. Will you stay on, dear, until you decide whether you want to go back to the State Department?"

"Well…"

Lowering her lashes, Gillian twirled the stem of her champagne flute between her fingers. She'd planned to wait to make her own announcement. Since Elizabeth had set the stage, however…

"Actually, I *am* staying on. As an agent."

"The hell you are!"

The explosive remark surprised everyone, including the operative it burst from. Red surged above the collar of Mike Callahan's shirt collar as all heads turned in his direction, but the frown he directed at Gillian was fierce and unapologetic.

She answered the thunderous scowl with one of her quick smiles. "It's a done deal. Uncle Nick gave his stamp of approval yesterday."

"Not without considerable arm twisting," her honorary uncle muttered under his breath.

Mike Callahan, code name Hawkeye, tightened his jaw. "You're not trained for this kind of work, Jilly."

"I'll get the training."

Gillian's smile took on an edge that either of her siblings would have recognized in a heartbeat. "I held my own in Scotland. Didn't I, Rogue?"

The tall, slender blonde she addressed nodded. "That you did, girlfriend."

Yeah, Callahan thought savagely. And he hadn't drawn a full breath until he'd put her on a plane for home.

A former military cop, he was a dead shot with every weapon in the government's arsenal and a good number that weren't. Hence his code name, Hawkeye, which most of his fellow agents shortened to Hawk. In his civilian life he was a marksmanship instructor at the Federal Law Enforcement Academy at Quantico, Virginia. He'd also taught all three of the Ridgeway off-spring to shoot.

Gillian-with-a-J had been the first. The *J* was a standing joke that went back to their initial meeting. All arms and long, long legs, the teenager had grinned up at him and introduced herself as Gillian, pronounced with a soft *G,* like in Jillian.

Hawk had lost part of his heart to the gangly teen right then and there. In the years since, he'd come damned close to losing the rest of it. Like most of the male agents at OMEGA, he was seriously in lust with the stunning, sensual creature Gillian Ridgeway had become. The woman could set off a firestorm in his belly with a single glance from those electric blue eyes.

He'd kept the fire in check, however. Despite the hints she'd been throwing his way recently, he knew damned well he was too old for her, too rough around the edges. He also knew that undercover work could be dangerous not only for him but for anyone who went into the field with him.

He looked at her now, his insides twisting as another

face superimposed itself on Gillian's classic features. He could hear the splat of bullets tearing through the vines. Feel the vicious downwash of the chopper hovering above the canopy. See the sprawled, lifeless body of the woman he'd gone into the jungle with.

Slamming the door on the searing memory, he swung toward Gillian's parents. "You've both been field agents. You know what it's like. You're good with this?"

"Yes," Maggie said instantly, then flashed an annoyed look when her husband gave a less enthusiastic response.

"I'll admit I'm not particularly thrilled with the idea," Adam said coolly, "but I trust Gillian's instincts."

Christ! Hawk's gut kinked again. Couldn't they see she lacked the killer instinct? She was too refined, too educated, too damned beautiful to…

The sudden buzz of the phone on Lightning's desk sliced into Hawk's chaotic thoughts. The blinking red light that accompanied the buzz stiffened his shoulders.

He and everyone else in the room knew that blinking light was the direct line to the White House…and that they should clear out of the director's office, fast. Depositing their champagne glasses, they made for the door.

Maggie and Adam could have stayed. They'd both taken direct calls from past presidents and were still cleared at the highest levels. But Lightning now shouldered responsibility for OMEGA. Unwilling to intrude on his turf, they joined the general exodus.

The operatives headed for the elevator that would whisk them to the ultra-high-tech Operations Center on the third floor of the town house. Hawk hesitated several seconds before he, too, strode toward the elevator.

Adam's eyes were narrowed as he followed the man's progress. Maggie's were thoughtful. Hooking her chin, she signaled for Jilly to accompany her to the ladies' room just off the first-floor foyer.

"Okay, daughter of mine." Leaning her hips against the marble counter, Maggie crossed her arms. "Tell me again, no frills, no fuss. How much of your decision to join OMEGA's ranks stems from a real desire to work undercover and how much from a determination to prove to Mike Callahan that you're all grown up?"

Jilly didn't blink. "I'm one hundred percent...on both counts."

Maggie eyed her daughter for long moments. She knew Hawk's paternalistic and overly protective attitude irritated Jilly no end. The irritation had increased exponentially since their trip to Scotland. Maggie thought of all the advice she could offer and reduced it to one caution.

"Don't push him too hard, Jilly. You might not like it when he pushes back."

Her daughter's jet-black brows snapped together. She looked so much like her father when he was annoyed that Maggie's heart kicked over.

"You and Dad have known Hawk for years. This is the first time you've ever hinted that you have a problem with him."

"We don't. We would trust him with our lives."

"But not with your daughter. What do you know about him that I don't?"

Maggie hooked a strand of golden-brown hair behind one ear, considering her answer. She'd cheerfully rip out the heart of anyone who threatened her husband or children. But she had to weigh that fierce, primal love against her loyalty to the men and women she'd lived, worked and sweated blood with for so many years.

"I don't know the details," she said slowly. "No one does. Hawk has never talked about why he left the military, but…"

"But?"

"Your father ran into his former commanding officer at some function or another. The general didn't go into specifics, but he did say Hawk hung up his uniform after a botched mission in Central America. Hawk went in with two other operatives. One of them didn't make it out. The general didn't say so but the implication was he buried his heart with her there in that steamy jungle."

"Her?" Jilly echoed softly. "That explains a lot."

"I thought it might. Tread carefully, sweetheart."

Maggie couldn't resist giving her daughter's silky black hair a gentle yank. Where was the wide-eyed toddler who'd pulled up the just-planted pansies to decorate her mudpies? What happened to the mischievous little girl who loved to dress an ungainly iguana in doll clothes, deposit him in her baby sister's buggy and stroll nonchalantly around the block? When had the giggling teen with braces grown into this smart, self-assured woman?

With a silent sigh, Maggie gave her daughter's hair another tug and shooed her out of the ladies' room. "You'd better go see what that call was about, Special Agent-in-Training Ridgeway."

She tried to contain her emotion as she watched Jilly make for the elevator, but her husband knew her too well.

"She'll be okay."

Adam forced a smile as he looked down into his wife's face, but acid rolled around in his stomach at the thought of what lay ahead of his darling, his little princess. He'd been out there. So had Maggie. Her exploits in the field had aged Adam well beyond his years. Remembering those turbulent times, his smile relaxed into a rueful grin.

"She'll be okay," he repeated. "She's her mother's daughter."

The atmosphere inside OMEGA's third-floor Control Center left no doubt in Jilly's mind. Something was up. Something big.

She'd been up to the busy Control Center any number of times while filling in for Elizabeth. But the realization that one of those amber lights on the digitized world map that took up an entire wall would soon represent her sent a shiver of excitement down her spine.

Most of the agents had already dispersed, some to milk OMEGA's computers, some to work the phones. Lightning stood at the main console with Hawk, their eyes glued to the data scrolling across a monitor.

They couldn't be more different, Jilly thought as she approached the two men. With his tawny hair, deep tan and sartorial elegance, Lightning looked very much like the sophisticated jet-setter he now was.

Mike Callahan, on the other hand, looked very much like the man *he* was. Tough, uncompromising, no nonsense. He was more rugged than handsome, with a square chin and a mouth that rarely smiled. He wore his dark brown hair cut military short. His gold-flecked hazel eyes missed little. So little that Jilly had always believed that's how he'd come by his code name of Hawkeye.

Until she'd seen him shoot, that is. The first time had been at an International Law Enforcement Tri-Gun Competition. Her parents had taken her to watch the final round, where Hawk scored top honors in the handgun and heavy metal categories. To his disgust, he'd come in second in the shotgun class. He rose to hero status in her eyes that day. She'd been trying to bring him down to the level of mere mortal ever since.

Soon, she vowed as both men acknowledged her arrival with a quick glance. Soon.

"What have we got?" she asked.

Her deliberate use of the plural produced a scowl from Hawk, but Lightning accepted her into the fold.

"Some sort of mutant virus," he replied in a grim voice. "Scientists at the U.S. Fish and Wildlife Service Forensics Lab found it a week ago when they autopsied the carcass of a…" He glanced at the computer monitor in front of him. "A *nomascus concolor*."

Jilly didn't even try to pretend she knew what that was.

"It's a monkey," Lightning informed her. "Or rather, a gibbon. A species of small ape native to southern China and Southeast Asia."

He swiveled the monitor around to display a black, furry creature with tufts of white on his cheeks and impossibly long arms.

"It's the most critically endangered ape species in the world. Supposedly, its very scarcity makes it highly prized as a sacrificial offering in certain far-out religious cults."

The tiny ape on the screen stared back at Jilly with an inquisitive expression in his caramel-colored eyes. The thought of this cuddly little creature being carved up by religious fanatics raised goose bumps on her skin.

"Someone tossed the carcass of one of these gibbons into a ditch in California," Lightning continued. "Both the road worker who discovered it and the animal-control officer who responded to his call are now in intensive care. Their docs are still trying to find the right combination of drugs to combat the virus infecting them."

That was scary. Gillian knew all kinds of nasty diseases like HIV, SARS and Ebola were linked to primates. Now, apparently, a new one had appeared on the scene.

"How did this gibbon get into the States?"

"We don't know. But the bug that killed it has proved so virulent that Homeland Security tasked one of their top agents to track down the person or persons who brought it in." Lightning's voice went flat and hard. "That agent was found this morning in a back alley in San Francisco, with a bone-handled knife through his throat."

His glance cut to the operative standing stone-faced and rigid on the other side of the communications console.

"Hawk was just about to tell us why his name was the last word the agent uttered."

The clatter of keyboards and hum of voices in the Control Center stilled. A tense silence descended until Hawk broke it with slow deliberation.

"Charlie Duncan and I served together. A long time ago. In Special Ops. He saved my life. My guess is he was hoping I'd repay the favor by hunting down whoever put that shiv through his throat."

His rigidly controlled tone belied the feral light in his hazel eyes. For the first time in her life, Jilly was just a little afraid of him.

Her mother's warning rang in her ears. But as quickly as the goosey feeling came, she shoved it aside. This was Mike Callahan. The man who'd cradled her against his chest, corrected her aim and taught her to put nine out of ten rounds dead center. He was big, certainly. Gruff, sometimes. Hot as hell, always. She refused to be afraid of a man she fully intended to bring to his knees.

Unaware of his fate, Hawk zeroed in on Lightning. "I want this mission."

"You've got it."

"I'll fly out to California tomorrow, see what leads the locals have on Charlie's death."

"You might want to talk to the folks at the Centers for Disease Control here in D.C. first."

"Will do."

"I can help," Jilly said. "I spent three years in Asia. I could…"

"No."

Hawk rounded on her.

"Listen to me, Gillian-with-a-J. We're talking a potentially lethal virus. Possibly radical religious nuts. A cold-blooded killer or killers. That's enough for me to handle without worrying about you running around playing amateur secret agent."

Heat rushed into Jilly's cheeks and fire into her eyes. Before she could let fly, Hawk raked a hand through his short-cropped hair and offered a grudging compromise.

"I don't like the idea of you getting into this game.

You know that. But… Well, it looks like you've made up your mind. I'll mentor you, Jilly. Teach you some of the tricks of the trade I've picked up over the years. After I get back from this mission. In the meantime, I need you to stay out of my way."

Mentoring was the last thing she wanted from Mike Callahan. This was hardly the time to tell him so, however.

"I'll stay out of your way," she promised, masking her anger with icy politeness, "but at least let me work my contacts at the State Department. They have a special desk tracking religious splinter groups. One of the analysts might have something we can use."

"All right, but let me know immediately if you find anything."

His tone implied that he was highly doubtful, and Jilly had to subdue a thoroughly unprofessional impulse to flip him the bird. The gesture would have been wasted in any case. He'd already turned his attention back to Lightning.

Chapter 2

Jilly steamed all the way to Foggy Bottom.

None of the other passengers on the Metro would have guessed she was pissed. She smiled her thanks to the tattooed kid who moved aside to give her room. She apologized to the Navy lieutenant she bumped into when the train took off. And she had herself well in hand when she exited the Metro and took the soaring escalator at the Foggy Bottom–George Washington University stop.

Foggy Bottom got its name from the mist that swirled through the low-lying area between the Potomac River and Rock Creek. The Bottom was home to a host of well-known institutions, including George Washington University, the Kennedy Center and the infamous Watergate Hotel. Most Washington pundits, however, believed the "fog" emanated from the government agency that took up an entire block on C Street.

The headquarters of the U.S. Department of State was a monolithic square of concrete and glass. Jilly could still remember the thrill that had danced through her when she mounted the front steps for the first time as a very new and very junior Foreign Service Officer. She suspected her father's considerable pull had something to do with her acceptance into the highly competitive Foreign Service. That, and acing the Foreign Service Officers' exam. The fact that she'd inherited her mother's flair for languages and had snagged a graduate Fulbright scholarship to study Mandarin at Peking University hadn't hurt, either.

Her linguistic skills had led to her first assignment as a cultural affairs officer in Beijing. Those three years had been exciting as hell but convinced Jilly she wasn't the stuff bureaucrats are made of. She'd loved the people she worked with and fully appreciated the positive effects of cultural exchanges but *hated* the paperwork.

She'd returned from Beijing undecided about a career with the State Department. The months she'd spent filling in for Elizabeth Wells had settled the matter. As an OMEGA operative, she could still travel to exotic locations, still engage with people of all nationalities and political persuasions. But she wouldn't have to write a twenty-page report after every contact.

Since she'd handed in her State Department ID along with her resignation, she had to wait at the visitors' entrance for an escort. He emerged from the inner sanctum moments later and greeted her in fluent Mandarin.

"*Nee hao,* Gillian. *Ching shou, nee huey lai dao State!*"

Laughing, she shook her head and answered in kind. "Sorry, Don. I'm not returning to the fold. I'm here as a civilian. And a supplicant."

Don Ackerman huffed in disappointment. He was one of several senior Foreign Service Officers who staffed the China desk. He'd tried every stratagem in his considerable repertoire to keep Jilly in his sector, including outright bribes and her choice of assignments.

"What can I do for you?" he asked after he'd signed her in and she'd processed through security screening.

"Point me to whoever's handling radical religious cults these days."

"You're kidding, right? You know very well two thirds of our antiterrorist division is working that threat."

"This one doesn't sound jihadist, unless they've gotten into animal sacrifice."

"Animal sacrifice?" Don scratched his chin and led the way down a long corridor. "We've got several of those. The most visible is the Santeria sect in south Florida. But the Supreme Court decided their ritual sacrifice of chickens during ceremonies is an expression of religious freedom, so we don't classify them as radical anymore."

"How about monkeys? Or small apes?"

Ackerman's lips pursed. He was a big man, going soft around the middle these days, but still possessed the encyclopedic knowledge of world cultures that had made him a legend at State.

"That sounds more like the Vhrana Sect." He came to a full stop in the hallway. "They're bad news, Gillian. What's your interest in them?"

Although she suspected State had received the same urgent missive Lightning had, Jilly hadn't been cleared to discuss it with anyone outside OMEGA. All she could tell Don was a basic version of the truth.

"I'm doing some research for the agency I now work for."

His penetrating gray eyes drilled into her. "You'd better talk to Sandra Hathaway. She's our Vhrana expert."

Sandra Hathaway was a dark-haired, intense analyst. The kind, Jilly guessed, who doled out information sparingly to folks in the field. She hunched over her computer and made no effort to disguise her annoyance at the interruption. Her irritation morphed instantly into a closed, guarded expression when Don mentioned the Vhrana.

He overrode her bureaucratic caution with a blunt order. "Gillian was one of our own until she bailed. Despite that serious lapse of judgment, I'll vouch for her. Give her whatever information you can about the sect."

"Whatever" turned out to be scary as hell. The Vhrana, Jilly soon learned, were an even more dangerous splinter group of the religious fanatics who set off chemical bombs in a Tokyo subway some years back.

"The Vhrana believe the only true path to enlightenment is to cleanse the world of evil, as they see it," Hathaway related. "They practice rites that derive from Buddhism and ancient forms of Hinduism, with a dash of Turkish Sufi thrown in. The more 'advanced' in the sect go into trances and spin around for hours."

"Like whirling dervishes?"

"Precisely."

"And they also practice animal sacrifice?"

"In ancient times, they sacrificed humans. Usually enemies captured after a battle. The Vhrana drank blood from the vanquished warriors' skulls to imbibe their valor before devouring their hearts and livers."

"Nice guys."

"Don't delude yourself. The women in the sect were—and still are—every bit as bloodthirsty. You don't want to get crosswise of a Vhrana priestess. Nowadays, of course, human sacrifice has been outlawed. So has animal sacrifice, for that matter, but the Vhrana still practice it on holy days. They're rumored to offer up a variety of animals, but their sacrifice of choice is a monkey or ape."

The picture of the little gibbon flashed into Jilly's mind.

"I thought most Hindus revere monkeys. In fact, I remember reading about the hordes of monkeys that now overrun New Delhi because the devout feed them peanuts and bananas."

"The Vhrana have perverted that reverence. Or elevated it, I guess you could say. Since primates are the closest things to humans, they believe they're honoring the animal by sacrificing them to their gods."

"Do you have a fix on the Vhrana sects in the U.S.?"

"We're tracking seven different branches. The largest is in California."

Where the dead gibbon was found. A frisson of excitement jumped along Jilly's nerves. She didn't have the training or field experience of a seasoned agent, but every scrap of intuition she possessed told her she was on the right trail.

"The second-largest sect is right across the state line,"

Hathaway continued, "in Baltimore. It draws most of its followers from the D.C. area." Swinging around, she clicked a few keys on her computer. "Here's a shot of the exterior of their temple."

Jilly studied the windowless brick building. "It looks like a warehouse."

"It is. We've ascertained that the owner has no idea what goes on in his building between the hours of midnight and dawn. His night manager takes over then."

Another click brought up a shot of a handsome man in the turban of a Sikh. Next to him was a smiling, doe-eyed female in a turquoise sari and veil.

"That's the night manager's wife, the current high priestess. We've been told she wields the knife at the altar. We hope to verify that tonight."

"Tonight?"

"It's the first night of the second full moon since harvest. One of their holiest days."

"Who's going in?"

"Special Agent Nareesh. He was one of us until he transferred to the FBI."

"Benjamin Nareesh?"

"Yes. You know him?"

"I do! We trained together as junior FSOs."

Her pulse tripping, Jilly got Nareesh's number from Sandra Hathaway.

The afternoon sun had warmed the air when she emerged from State. She stood for some moments on the wide front steps, debating her next step. She really, really wanted to follow this lead on her own. If it produced results, Hawk would have to eat his objections to her lack of training and experience. Common sense and the awareness that she was part of a team had her reaching for her cell phone.

Since she hadn't yet been equipped with one of OMEGA's handy-dandy, supersecure communications devices, she couldn't directly access the Control Center or any of the operatives. Instead, she dialed the number for Lightning's executive assistant.

"Offices of the Special Envoy. How may I help you?"

"Elizabeth, it's Jilly. I need to speak to Uncle Nick."

"He's still in conference, dear."

In conference was code for upstairs, doing duty as OMEGA's director.

"I thought he might be. Ask him to call me on my cell when he's free."

Her cell phone pinged moments later.

"Where are you, Jilly?"

"Just leaving State. I may have something."

Or not. The lead was pretty tenuous at this point.

"I want your okay to accompany a friend on a visit to a temple tonight." She couldn't go into more detail over an open line. "I'll brief you after the visit."

The silence on the other end was deafening.

"Are you sure you know what you're doing?" Lightning finally asked.

"No, but my friend does. He's with the Bureau. His boss might call you for confirmation that it's okay for me to ride along. Will you give it?"

Another silence, longer this time.

"Uncle Nick? Am I good to go?"

"You're good."

She restrained her exultant whoop but couldn't resist punching the air with her fist.

Hours later, she huddled beside a turbaned Ben Nareesh in his darkened car. Their intent gazes were fixed on the small screen in his handheld unit. It was fed by cameras the FBI had positioned to cover the brick warehouse. Figures had been slipping through the cloudy night and into the warehouse for the past half hour.

"I still can't believe I let you talk me into this," Nareesh muttered. "Or that my boss gave the green light. You must have some powerful contacts."

Jilly merely smiled as Ben's gaze swept over her, looking for a chink in her disguise.

He didn't find one. She was draped in a silk sari she'd purchased in a downtown D.C. shop that catered to the city's large Indian and Pakistani population. Tinted contacts darkened her eyes. Thankfully, her jet-black hair had needed no touching up. She'd parted it in the middle and fashioned an intricate series of braids that now tugged at her scalp.

"Just follow my lead," he instructed. "And if we do find any sacrificial animals, we both stay the hell away from them."

Ben hadn't taken her warning about a potentially lethal virus lightly. In addition to his team of backups, he now had a crew encased in biohazard protective gear standing ready. All were prepared to move at his signal.

Jilly's nerves were strung tight when Ben stowed his unit and shifted to face her.

"Ready?"

She hooked the silk veil across the lower half of her face, dragged in a deep breath and nodded.

"Ready."

Hawk was huddled with a team of scientists at the Centers for Disease Control's Washington office when a cell phone chimed.

"That's mine." Annoyed at the interruption, the woman opposite Hawk flipped open her phone. "Dr. Cook."

He could tell the news was electrifying. The doc jolted upright in her chair and whipped a startled gaze his way before snapping the phone shut.

"The FBI just raided some kind of underground temple. One of the folks on the raid wanted to know if you're still here."

Hawk's insides turned to ice. Jilly. That had to be Jilly.

"They found several animals being prepared for sacrifice. One of them is an extremely rare *nomascus concolor*. The team has the animals in isolation units. They're delivering them to the containment lab as we speak."

All three scientists were already out of their chairs. Hawk stayed right on their heels as they raced through a maze of darkened corridors, down three flights of stairs and through an underground tunnel to a brightly lit lab.

He'd had to accept that Lightning had given her the go-ahead to accompany this friend of hers. A thorough check of Special Agent Nareesh's background and credentials had resolved some of Hawk's misgivings. That, and the fact that she would just ride along. As an observer. Not a direct participant.

He was still nursing that mistaken notion when he picked up the wail of a siren.

"Stay in the observation booth," Dr. Cook instructed as she zipped herself into biohazard protective gear. "It's sealed off and safe."

The booth's glass wall gave Hawk a clear view of the team that entered the lab some moments later. Looking like space travelers in their hooded suits, the team carried plastic cages with controlled breathing units. One of the cages contained what looked like a small rhesus monkey, the other a slightly larger primate with white tufts of fur on its cheeks. The gibbon's eyes were huge and frightened and seemed to lock on Hawk through the glass window.

"Poor babies."

He recognized Jilly's voice instantly but had to look twice to ID the woman who rushed into the booth, followed by a tall, slender man in a white turban.

Black mascara rimmed her eyes, which looked decidedly not blue from where he stood. A red caste mark decorated her forehead. To go with the pistachio green sari draped across one shoulder, he surmised, and sweet, cloying scent of incense that surrounded her like a cloud.

"Hawk! They told me you were still here. This is Special Agent Ben Nareesh. Ben, this is Mike Callahan."

She paused, smiled and looked Hawk square in the eye and said, "Mike and I work together."

Hawk got the message. In her own, inimitable way, Gillian-with-a-J had just thrown down the gauntlet. If he didn't accept her as an equal, right here, right now, it would be war between them.

He knew he would come out the victor. He fought too dirty to be vanquished by a pampered, privileged country-club type. Except Gillian Ridgeway, for all her pampering and privilege, possessed some real smarts under that sleek, silky mane. And she had the guts to match. She'd proven that tonight.

With a wrench that took him back to a place he never wanted to go again, Hawk yielded the field and extended a hand to Nareesh. "Good to meet you."

He couldn't miss Jilly's flash of triumph. It stayed on her face until she turned back to the observation window.

"They won't hurt them, will they?"

After his session with the folks at the Center, Hawk had a pretty good idea what might happen to the primates. It wasn't pretty.

"Depends on whether they show signs of infection."

"If they don't?"

"I don't know. They might be used for testing or research. Or turned over to a zoo," he added as Jilly's brows snapped together.

"Poor babies," she muttered again. "I wonder…"

Her lips pursed, and her expression turned thoughtful. Hawk had a sudden vision of Jilly showing up at the Ridgeway place with two hairy primates in tow. Maggie wouldn't mind. He could only imagine Adam's reaction.

"Ben, promise you'll keep me posted on what happens to these little guys."

Her request took the FBI agent by surprise. Obviously, he'd assumed his responsibility for the animals ended with the raid.

"I…uh…sure."

The man was putty in Jilly's hands.

Join the club, Hawk thought sardonically.

"Or," Nareesh countered in an attempt to wiggle out of the charge, "you could probably get the folks here at the Center to advise you directly."

"I could, if my partner and I weren't leaving for Hong Kong as soon as we throw a few things in a bag."

Enough was enough. Goaded, Hawk hooked her arm and swung her around. "Damn it, Gillian. How many surprises are you planning to pull tonight?"

"Sorry."

Her contrite look didn't fool him for a minute.

"I should have mentioned it right away. One of the worshippers arrested in the raid told us how the sacrificial animals were smuggled into the States."

She paused, playing the info for all it was worth. Hawk had to concede she'd earned her moment of glory.

"They were hidden inside a shipping container packed with antiques exported from Hong Kong. The shipping agency is Wang and Company."

Behind her tinted contacts, her eyes held only limpid innocence.

"Unless your Chinese is better than mine, Hawk, you might want to reconsider whether or not I'll be in the way when you call on Mr. Wang."

Chapter 3

Early the next morning, Hawk contacted the San Francisco detectives investigating Charlie Duncan's murder. They had no witnesses, no suspects and no leads. Frustrated, he used the remaining hours before he and Jilly departed for Hong Kong to supervise her transition from one-time Foreign Service Officer and temporary executive assistant to full-fledged undercover operative.

Jilly discovered a new Mike Callahan during those hours. This one was impatient, demanding and absolutely relentless. He began in OMEGA's training center with a crash course in down-and-dirty offensive and defensive maneuvers. Jilly was drenched with sweat and sporting several nasty bruises before she finally managed a takedown.

Hawk didn't allow her time for so much as a smirk to celebrate. Rolling to his feet, he hustled her into the weapons facility. He'd taught her to shoot, knew she could handle the polymer-based Beretta Sub-Compact she'd carry on this mission. Still, he made her snap in a clip and shred several paper targets before he turned her over to OMEGA's communications team.

Despite her grungy gray sweats and sweat-flattened hair, Jilly paid close attention while the team drilled her on communications procedures. Her only break came when Mackenzie Blair, Lightning's wife and the guru of all things electronic for OMEGA and several other government agencies, marched in.

"Well, my sweet, you certainly didn't waste any time snagging your first field op."

"What can I say? Duty calls."

Raking back her limp hair, Jilly grinned at the brunette she considered more of a big sister than an honorary aunt.

"How's the baby?"

Mac rounded a hand over her prominent belly and made a face. "The little stinker sleeps all day and kicks all night. Want to see what I have for you?"

Both women instantly switched gears. Mac's high-tech devices had made her a legend with the agencies she supplied. Jilly couldn't wait to see what supercool, James Bondish gadget she'd come up with this time.

It didn't look all that high-tech at first. The gold charm was pretty, though. It was in the shape of a Chinese character and embedded in a bezel of what looked like rare blue jade.

"Do you know this character?" Mac asked.

"Fu. It means good luck." Jilly had to laugh. "Appropriate."

"I thought so, too. This particular Fu, my sweet, just happens to conceal the world's smallest and most sophisticated encrypted satellite communications system."

With her belly nudging the table, Mac laid the charm in the palm of one hand and poked at it with the other.

"If you press on this little squiggle…"

"That squiggle is the character's radical, or root symbol."

After four years of Mandarin in college, two more in grad school and a three-year tour of duty in Beijing, Jilly spoke several Chinese dialects with a fluency rarely acquired by "foreign devils."

Reading and writing were entirely different matters. By various counts, there were somewhere between forty and fifty thousand Chinese characters. Thankfully, each character contained one of only two hundred and fourteen roots. If you could figure out the root, you could count the character's remaining strokes and— most of the time!—look up the word in a dictionary.

"The roots came down from ancient times," she told Mac. "Originally they were pictographs representing basic elements like man, woman, fire, water, and so on."

"If you say so. Press the root…radical…whatever…once to transmit, twice to receive. Go ahead, try a voice transmission."

Jilly pressed once. "Mary had a little… Whoa!"

She jumped as the nursery rhyme boomed through the Control Center's speakers.

"You'll be in silent mode most of the time," Mac advised, "but you'll know when someone's trying to contact you. Put it on, and I'll give you a demo."

The chain was long enough to loop easily over her head. The jade felt cool and smooth against her throat—until Mac signaled to one of her assistants. The next moment, the semiprecious stone warmed like toast.

"Nice," Jilly murmured, palming the charm. "Very nice."

"It's also equipped with GPS, an electronic jammer and a direct link to Hawk's comm unit."

"Don't tell me you decked him out in a gold chain and charm, too?"

"I wish! No, his comm is in his watch." A wicked gleam lit Mac's brown eyes. "But I did spiffy that up to go with your cover. You should have seen his face when I presented him with a solid gold Rolex."

Also appropriate, Jilly thought. She and Hawk would hit Hong Kong in the guise of a wealthy couple on a Far East buying junket.

A *married* couple.

Sharing a hotel suite.

So Hawk could keep an eye on her.

She'd bristled at that last bit. Not for long, however, since adjoining bedrooms in a luxurious hotel suite dovetailed nicely with her non-mission-related objectives.

Assuming she didn't pull out her Beretta and pump a round into Hawk before they left for Hong Kong, which she seriously contemplated doing an hour later.

Not content with her firm grasp of OMEGA's internal communications codes, Hawk insisted she memorize the NATO phonetic alphabet used by police officers and medical response agencies worldwide. That Jilly could rattle the letters off with some assurance wasn't enough. He wanted every one burned into her subconscious.

"Give them to me again."

She gritted her teeth. "How many times do I have to…?"

"Again, damn it." The gold flecks in his eyes burned with intensity. "I'm not going into the field with someone who can't call for backup if we run into an ambush."

Was that what happened all those years ago in the jungle? Had Hawk and his partner and this woman he once loved been ambushed? The thought of what he'd lost in that murky green darkness put a lid on Jilly's irritation.

"Alpha-Bravo-Charlie-Delta-Echo-Foxtrot-Golf-Hotel-India-Juliet-Kilo-Lima-Mike."

She pulled in a breath.

"November-Oscar-Papa-Quebec-Romeo-Sierra-Tango-Uniform-Victor-Whiskey-Xray-Yankee-Zulu."

She finished on a whoosh of air and gave him a nasty glare.

"Satisfied?"

"Yeah."

He didn't look satisfied. With his two-day's worth of stubble and red-rimmed eyes, he looked almost as ragged as she now felt.

"We've got less than an hour before we have to head for the airport," he informed her after checking his gleaming Rolex. "We'd better get up to Field Dress."

Finally! A shower, a shampoo and a quick blow-dry.

She couldn't wait to shed her rank sweats and change into whatever the wizards in OMEGA's Field Dress Unit had waiting for her.

Gillian emerged from FDU's dressing room a different woman. Nothing like a French silk demibra and panties, an Emanuel Ungaro pantsuit in cobalt-blue and Bruno Magli ankle boots to make a gal feel like she could take on the world again. She'd have to wait until Hong Kong to see the other delights packed in the Gucci suitcases waiting beside the dressing room door.

Hawk was waiting, as well. His gaze raked her from head to toe. A small grunt was her only indication that her duty uniform passed inspection. She, on the other hand, could barely keep her jaw from dropping.

She'd known him for so long, had seen him rigged out in everything from camouflage gear to a hand-tailored tux. But this was the first time she'd *ever* seen him with his brown hair slicked back and his nails manicured. Or in an Armani sport coat that molded his wide shoulders. Or Italian leather loafers. Or...

"If you're through conducting your inventory," he said impatiently, "we need to hit the road."

She popped a salute. "Yes, sir! It's just that... You look so different."

The Field Dress tech who'd outfitted them both frowned. "Not too different, I hope."

After discussing the matter with Lightning, Hawk had decided he should stick to his civilian persona. He was too well-known in the international marksmanship circuit to do otherwise. But his recent marriage to a wealthy heiress had plucked him from the shooting range and plunged him into the world of manicures and priceless artifacts. Or so he and Jilly would pretend.

With a spurt of real glee, she contemplated the crash course in Oriental antiques she would subject *him* to during the long flight to Hong Kong.

"I'm ready if you are," she told him.

"Not quite. We have one more piece of business to take care of."

She couldn't hold back a groan. "Not more codes!"

"Just one. You haven't picked your code name."

"We've been going nonstop since dawn. Who had time to think names?"

"So think now. What, or who, are you?"

"I don't know."

"We need a name, Jilly."

Fiddling with the pendant that nestled just above the swell of her breasts, she searched her mind.

"I can't come up with… Wait!" She stroked her thumb over the smooth round bezel. "Jade. I'll go by Jade."

Hawk's expression softened. For a moment, just a moment, she was sure she caught the ghost of a grin on his rugged face.

"Is that with a *G* or a *J?*"

"J." She smiled back.

"I'll let Griff know."

Dan Griffin, code name Ace, would act as their controller during this op. Only a few years older than Jilly, the former Navy pilot with the killer grin had already made a name for himself at OMEGA…and with the women who couldn't seem to get enough of him.

Hawk made a half turn and swung back to Jilly. "One more thing. You'd better put this on."

He dug in the pocket of his Armani jacket and withdrew a jeweler's box. When he popped the lid, Jilly gasped. Nested in velvet was a circlet of marquise-cut diamonds banded by sapphire-studded ring guards.

"It's gorgeous."

"Yeah. Field Dress doesn't miss a trick."

Her heart stuttered and almost stopped when he slid the wide band onto her ring finger. Cover, she reminded herself with a gulp. This was strictly for cover.

Which didn't explain why Hawk kept her hand in his for several seconds longer.

"I told them I wanted the ring guards in sapphire. To match your eyes."

She pondered that gruff comment all the way across the Pacific.

Hong Kong was everything she remembered from shopping excursions during her assignment to Beijing. And more. So much more.

As their plane swooped in for a landing, Jilly saw dozens of new skyscrapers crowding the harbor on both Hong Kong Island and the Kowloon Peninsula on the mainland. Contrary to the dire predictions when the British relinquished their hold on the territories known collectively as Hong Kong, their teeming economy hadn't collapsed. Instead, it was exploding.

Gillian soon discovered that the traffic she recalled from previous visits had exploded, as well. Their limo driver added frequent blasts of his horn to the cacophony rising from taxis, trucks and Japanese-made vehicles of every sort. Masses of humanity, most with cell phones jammed against their ears, thronged streets with signs in both English and Chinese. Narrow alleys radiated from avenues with names left over from the British occupation. Sheng Tung Street bisected Waterloo Road. Kam Lam ran into Argyle. Tak Shing, Kan Su and Nanking all converged on the shopaholic's mecca, Nathan Road.

Jilly almost salivated as the Rolls-Royce limo glided past shop after shop. She would have loved to put herself into the eager hands of tailors who could take her measurements and deliver an entire collection of suits and shoes and ball gowns to her hotel the next day. Or the jewelers who could craft an exquisite pair of diamond earrings or a ruby slide to her specifications within hours.

Then there were the designers. Prada, Chanel, Versace and Kate Spade all had boutiques on Nathan Road, as well as in the high-end malls scattered throughout the city. Too bad the Gucci suitcases stowed in the trunk of the Rolls-Royce made those boutiques and jewelry stores superfluous. Not to mention the ring on her left hand.

She snuck a glance at the sparkling stones. She hadn't gotten used to their weight yet. Or the odd sensation that came with even a pretend marriage to a man like Hawk.

Women always sat up and took notice when he entered a room. Their admiring glances had never bothered Jilly before. So she couldn't explain her annoyance with the redhead who'd almost tripped over her own feet while ogling Hawk at the airport. Or her irritation when a certain flight attendant became a little *too* attentive.

"That's the Peninsula ahead, sir."

The uniformed chauffeur pulled up at a red light and tipped his head toward the venerable hotel dominating the next block.

"Unfortunately, construction of the new subway line has temporarily blocked vehicle access to our main entrance. I'll have to let you out at the side entrance."

Well, darn! The Peninsula was one of Hong Kong's most revered institutions. Jilly had wanted Hawk to see the front portico with its massive white pillars, liveried doormen and fleet of Rolls-Royces at the ready. On impulse, she grabbed the door handle.

"Let's walk from here. The driver can drop off our bags at the side entrance. I want you to get the Peninsula's full effect."

The noise of a large and vibrant city hit them the moment they emerged from the Rolls. Car horns honked. Street vendors hawked their wares. Jackhammers and cranes added their signature sounds to the solid mass of humanity that thronged the streets. And above the din, Jilly caught the whistle of an arriving Star Ferry.

"You have to see this."

With a quick change in direction, she joined the crowd crossing the street. A short flight of steps led to the wide promenade that circled the Kowloon side of the Victoria Harbor.

Across the gray-green waters were the towering skyscrapers of Hong Kong Island. Victoria Peak rose above the columns of glass and steel, her summit wreathed in hazy mist. And there, just pulling into the terminal, was one of the distinctive green-and-white ferries that still served as a primary means of transportation.

Smiling at the sight, Jilly leaned her arms on the promenade's rail and breathed in the mingled scent of salt water and diesel fumes.

"They built a high-speed tunnel to connect Kowloon and Hong Kong some years ago," she told Hawk, "but I always take the ferries when I'm here. They're crowded, noisy and swarming with pickpockets, but they're quintessential China."

"I'll remember that."

Hawk obviously had more important matters on his mind as he shot back his cuff and checked his Rolex. "We'd better get settled in at the hotel, then call on Mr. Wang."

Jilly gave the magnificent skyline across the bay a last look and pushed away from the rail. Hawk put a hand to the small of her back to turn her toward the stairs. She shouldn't have felt his touch through layers of Hermès and Emanuel Ungaro. Shouldn't have but did. The skin under those layers tingled even as she issued another stern reminder.

Cover, girl! It's just cover!

Preoccupied with both the thought and the touch, she didn't see the pint-size street vendor in pink sneakers and T-shirt who'd approached them. Neither did Hawk until his abrupt turn brought them into direct contact.

"Ai-ah!"

The girl—she couldn't have been more than four or five—landed on her bottom. The wooden cage she was carrying also hit the concrete. The cage door flew open, and the canary inside made its escape.

With another cry, the girl scrambled to her feet and tried to catch the bird, but it was already soaring on the stiff breeze off the bay. Jilly would have bet the thing would soon be gull bait if she hadn't witnessed a similar performance during a previous visit to Hong Kong. That one had involved caged crickets, but the theatrics were the same.

Sure enough, the little girl's shoulders slumped pathetically. When she turned back to face them, tears rolled down her cheeks.

"I'm sorry, kid." Hawk reached into his pocket and pulled out the wad of Hong Kong dollars he'd purchased at the airport. "I'm really sorry."

"You might want to wait on that," Jilly advised.

"I bowled her over. How much should I give her for the bird? Five? Ten?"

"What you do to Mei Lin?"

The indignant query came from the boy who charged up the promenade stairs two at a time. He was older than the girl. Nine, maybe ten. Like her, he wore jeans and a faded T-shirt of indeterminate origin. But his AirMax Nikes, Jilly noted, looked brand-new.

"What you do?" he demanded again, but didn't wait for an answer. Waving his skinny arms, he launched into a tirade of broken English. "You hurt little sister. You break cage. She lose bird, lose money. Lose face with Grandfather."

The girl's tears continued to flow, and the boy's accusations were starting to attract attention.

"Here, kid. Will this save your sister's face?"

No fool, the boy took the twenty and held it up to the sunlight. Counterfeit money was as pandemic in China as bootlegged DVDs and Prada knockoffs.

The boy didn't lose his angry scowl, but his message to the girl held smug triumph. "We plucked a fat goose," he said in swift Cantonese. "Come, we'll buy hot dumplings to take to Grandfather."

Jilly said nothing while he scooped up the empty wooden cage. The two took off without another word and disappeared behind the oleanders separating the section of the promenade from the next.

Obviously relieved that the fracas was over, Hawk pocketed the rest of his money. "Let's go."

"Hang on a sec."

"Why?"

"Just listen. Yep, there it is."

The chirpy trill carried clearly over the hubbub of the harbor. A moment later, a flash of yellow nose-dived into the oleanders.

The man beside her was silent for several moments. "I knew it was a scam."

"Uh-huh." Grinning, Jilly hooked her arm through his. "You're on my turf now, fella. You might want to consult me before forking over any more twenty-dollar bills."

Hawk was a whole lot more concerned with his body's instant, instinctive reaction to the press of her breasts against his bicep than the fact that he'd been gulled by a couple of con artists.

What was with him, for God's sake? He'd held her in his arms before. And not just at the firing range. A few months ago, he'd escorted her to a black-tie reception and used her as cover while scoping out a congressman suspected of selling government secrets. He'd nailed his target, but sweat still gathered at the base of his spine when he remembered how Gillian-with-a-J had moved in a strapless, flame-colored column of silk that bared more of her than it covered.

Damn it all to hell! He had to get his head straight. Too much rode on this op to let his fantasies about this blue-eyed siren override his common sense.

"Let's go," he repeated with a distinct edge to his voice. "We have business to take care of."

Chapter 4

The first item on the agenda was to check into the hotel. Hawk was too preoccupied to appreciate the British colonial ambiance of the Peninsula's pillared entrance or the soaring lobby with its brass fixtures, rattan chairs and potted palms. Jilly, however, drank in the elegance as they walked to the reception desk.

"Welcome to the Peninsula, Mrs. Callahan."

With a small jolt, she realized the clerk at the reception desk had addressed her. "Thank you."

"I hope your flight in wasn't too exhausting."

"Not at all."

Once Hawk had stopped drilling her on operating procedures and let her get some sleep that is. She'd retaliated during the final leg of their journey with a lecture covering four thousand years of Chinese dynastic history.

"Is this your first trip to Hong Kong?"

"I've visited several times before but my…er…husband hasn't."

Hawk covered the near stumble by sliding an arm around her waist. "Still takes some getting used to, doesn't it, darling?"

His slow smile ignited sparks just under Jilly's skin and darned near melted the receptionist where she stood. Like hopeless romantics everywhere, the young woman got all googly-eyed. "Are you on your honeymoon?"

"We are."

"Congratulations." Her fingers tapped the keyboard. "Perhaps we might be able to switch you to the… Oh, I see you're already booked into one of our finest suites. I'll send up some champagne and fresh strawberries, compliments of the house."

"Sounds wonderful. We'll put them to good use."

There was that smile again. Tender, intimate, so full of sensual promise that heat raced through her like a California wildfire.

"Your luggage has already been taken up to your suite. If you'll just sign the registration form, Mr. Callahan, I'll scan your passports and credit card."

She didn't question the fact that Jilly's passport was in her maiden name. The blushing new bride wouldn't have had time to change it.

"You're in the Tower, sir. Edward will show you the way. And once again, my congratulations."

"Thanks."

As they followed the uniformed attendant to the elevators, Hawk kept the pretense up—and the wildfires raging—with a casually possessive hand to the small of Jilly's back.

The heat didn't cool until they reached the twenty-second floor and their escort slid a key card into a lock.

"There are two entrances to your suite," he informed them. "This one accesses the foyer. The other, just there, takes you into the walk-in closet and storage area."

Jilly thought that was pretty handy until she saw Hawk eyeing the second door with a crease between his brows. Two entrances, she realized belatedly, meant twice the necessary security precautions.

Damn! She'd better start thinking more like a field agent.

"Here you are."

Handing Hawk the key card, the attendant stood aside to let them precede him into the foyer. All marble and cream, with an artistic arrangement of snowy-white chrysanthemums on a side table, the entryway led into living and dining rooms that blended Asian and European with flawless symmetry.

Rich, jewel-toned Oriental rugs softened the parquet floors. Jilly's heels sank into the plush thickness as she admired the twin black lacquer chests inlaid with mother-of-pearl that framed the fireplace. The mantel held an artistic display of porcelain ginger jars in a delicate blue-and-white pattern that complimented the wingback chairs and sofas.

But it was the terrace with its floor-to-ceiling sliding-glass doors that knocked the breath back down her throat. Shedding her jacket, she aimed straight for the doors. Once outside she felt as though she was standing at the top of the world.

A stiff breeze whipped her hair while she watched gulls circling above a fishing junk that chugged through the gray-green waters of the bay. Across the harbor, late-afternoon sunlight glinted on the glass towers of Hong Kong. Twenty stories below, a cruise ship was just pulling into a berth alongside the Ocean Terminal.

"Hawk! Come see this view!"

When he didn't answer, she turned and found him with a phone already held to his ear.

"Guess the honeymoon is over," she murmured to the squawking gulls.

"That's right," Hawk was saying when she slid the terrace doors shut behind her. "Mr. and Mrs. Michael Callahan. We e-mailed Mr. Wang about arranging shipment of the furniture and antiques we intend to purchase in Hong Kong."

With one ear tuned to the phone conversation, Jilly went to explore the other rooms. Both sumptuous bedrooms boasted spectacular views of the skyline. So did the two bathrooms. Even the marble hot tub was set in a window enclosure with tall, angled windows that gave a sweeping, two-hundred-and-seventy-degree vista.

Their bags, she noted, had been laid on side-by-side racks in the walk-in luggage storage area that adjoined the master bath and dressing room. Hawk's raisin-colored leather suit bag hung next to her designer bag. The sight sent a sizzle of anticipation along Jilly's nerve endings.

She'd nursed a teenage crush on Mike Callahan for

years and had flirted with him all through college. He'd been so much a part of her life—the cool older guy with a string of international marksmanship awards she would brag about to her friends.

Her three years in Beijing had put some distance between them. Conversely, it had also compressed the years that separated them. Hawk was still the cool older guy in her mind, but she was long past girlish crushes and playful flirtations.

She ran her fingertips over the soft leather, thinking, planning, plotting her next move in this…

"Wang's not available."

Hastily, Jilly dropped her hand.

"We're meeting with his partner," Hawk said, striding in from the living room. "Her name's Hall. Adriana Hall. British, from the little I could glean. I've got OMEGA control checking her out."

"What time is the meeting?"

"Forty-five minutes from now. I've ordered a car. We'll have to leave in fifteen."

"Fifteen!"

She swallowed a groan as he retrieved her tote and his overnighter from the luggage room. So much for all her plotting and planning. The hot tub would have to wait. So would any "accidental" glimpses Hawk might snare of the sexy underwear Field Dress had procured for her.

"Which bedroom do you want?" he asked, bags in hand.

Separate bedrooms hadn't factored into her plotting, either. She mulled the matter over for a few seconds before responding.

"Word is going to spread among the hotel staff that we're on our honeymoon. Especially when they send up that champagne." She gave him her best secret-agent shrug. "It'll be tough to maintain our cover if we occupy separate bedrooms."

His eyes narrowed at the comment. Or maybe it was the shrug. Jilly wasn't sure she'd pulled that off.

"You think the black marketeers we're hunting have bribed the staff to spy on us?"

"Maybe not yet," she conceded. "But they might if they hear we're sniffing around, asking questions about them."

She didn't elaborate. Hawk had been in the business a whole lot longer than her day and a half. He had to know that a fistful of Hong Kong dollars could buy any interested party all kinds of information about the couple sharing this opulent suite. Like what they ordered from room service. Whether they preferred the foam pillows to feather. How many foil wrappers ended up in the wastebasket each night.

Heat jolted through her, fast and hot. With some effort, Jilly suppressed the image of Mike Callahan, tall and lean and naked except for a condom.

"You decide how we should play it while I'm in the bathroom."

Hawk didn't move for several moments after the door whisked shut behind her. He'd been so wrapped up in prepping Jilly for this mission—and so intent on getting to Wang and Company once they arrived in Hong Kong—that he'd shoved everything else into a separate compartment in his mind.

Jilly had just sprung that compartment wide-open. The mere thought of her slender body stretched next to his got Hawk hard. So hard that he had to clamp his jaw against the sudden urge to follow her into the bathroom and give the hotel staff some fuel for the fire.

Oh, for God's sake! What fire?

Smothering an oath, he forced himself to think rationally. They didn't need such deep cover. Not yet. The nameless, faceless smugglers they were hunting had to know another agent would pick up the investigation interrupted by Charlie Duncan's murder. But unless Hawk got sloppy and tipped his hand, the smugglers didn't know *he* was that agent. Or that he had a neophyte in tow.

The oath was more vicious this time. Stalking into the living room, Hawk threw his carryall atop the ornately carved rosewood desk. If Jilly got hurt, if she took a bullet and went down…

She wouldn't, he vowed savagely. Whatever it took, whatever lies he had to tell or protective walls he had to erect, he'd keep her out of the line of fire. He wasn't going to leave another piece of his heart lying in some back alley or dark, smothering jungle.

His jaw set, he unzipped his carryall and extracted a folded kit. The intrusion detection discs inside the kit were smaller than a dime, wafer thin and completely transparent. The recorder that went with them looked and acted like an iPod. With eighty gigs of memory, it could hold ten thousand songs, hundreds of JPEGs, downloaded movies and recent TV shows, as well as a whole address book full of contact information and a busy executive's calendar. After MacKenzie Blair and her magicians went to work on it, the device also contained a security system that would have made the folks at Fort Knox sit up and take notice.

Hawk attached one of the transparent discs above the transom of the door to the foyer, another above the luggage room door. He didn't like this double entry. He would have to plan for a worst-case scenario involving simultaneous assaults. On the other hand, the back door could provide an escape route for Jilly, if necessary.

Not particularly reassured by the thought, he attached additional discs to the terrace doors. Long habit had him opening a desk drawer a mere sliver. He also shifted one of the ginger jars gracing the tall Chinese chests a few inches to the left. A single glance would tell if someone had gone through the desk or lifted the lid to the chest.

The toiletries and wardrobe Field Dress had provided got the same careful attention. Hawk snagged his leather suit bag from the luggage area, intending to hang the items in his bedroom closet in precise order…and found himself right back where he'd started ten minutes ago.

Together, or separate? Honeymooners, or not?

"Hell!"

Stalking into the master bedroom, he yanked open the closet doors. He returned a few moments later for Jilly's hang-up and suitcase.

If she noted the side-by-side garment bags when she emerged from the bathroom and joined Hawk in the living room, she had the good sense not to comment on them.

"I'm all set." Her glance snagged on a silver ice bucket and domed tray. "Oh, good! The strawberries and champagne."

Not just strawberries, she saw when she lifted the lid. The sumptuous arrangement also included crystallized brown sugar and a creamy sauce for dipping.

"We need to go," Hawk insisted. "I'll put the tray in the fridge. You can feast tonight."

Jilly managed to snag one plump berry and a quick dip. Her taste buds gave a collective gasp of joy at the first bite. The sauce was white chocolate flavored with Grand Marnier. She polished off the berry in three bites.

"Did Control get back to you on Wang's partner?" she asked when Hawk returned.

"They did. You've got white stuff on your lower lip."

She swiped her tongue along her lip. "All gone?"

"Not quite. Here, let me."

His thumb brushed her mouth. Once. Twice. Jilly looked up, saw herself reflected in his eyes. She saw something else, something that made her breath catch. It came and went so fast that Hawk didn't give her time to feast on it.

"Let's go. I'll brief you on Adriana Hall during the drive."

"She's English," he confirmed as a gleaming Rolls-Royce whisked them through the tunnel connecting the Kowloon and Hong Kong Island. "According to Control, she's Wang's silent partner. Has been for several years."

A glass partition separated them from the chauffeur. The Rolls' incredible engineering blocked all tunnel noise and fumes. Traffic was light for Hong Kong and moved fast.

"She was married to Sir Reginald Hall. Control is still working him, but initial indications are he's descended from Singapore's last colonial governor. There were no children from the marriage. Sir Reginald's wife got into the antiquities trade in Singapore, then shifted her base of operations to Hong Kong after his death."

He drummed his fingers on his knee. Jilly waited, sensing he had more.

"There's a gap," Hawk confirmed. "Almost eight months between the time Hall died and his widow bought in as Wang's silent partner."

"Maybe she needed to adjust to losing her husband?"

"Maybe. The silent partner bit bothers me, though. Although Hong Kong reverted to China more than twenty years ago, old mystiques die hard. You'd think a savvy businesswoman would cash in on her connection to a peer of the British Empire."

Jilly fiddled with the jade pendant. Hawk's point was valid. Parts of Hong Kong still had something of a colonial air about them. Street names such as Argyle and Hamilton and Nathan Road were one example. This gleaming Rolls-Royce was another. But she could understand why a grieving widow might want to maintain a low profile.

She'd met a good number of British matrons over the years, first through her parents' international connections, then through her work as a cultural exchange officer at the U.S. Embassy in Beijing. The women she'd encountered exemplified the stiff upper lip the Brits were so famous for.

This one, this Adriana Hall, was probably cut from

the same cloth. She would carry on through adversity, all the while wrapping her grief in a cloak of privacy.

The woman whose twelfth-story office they entered a little later blew Jilly's ideas of British matrons all to hell.

This one looked as rare and exotic as the priceless antiques displayed in lighted niches around her office. Blond and slender, she was at least five-eight or -nine, although her three-inch stiletto heels accounted for some of that willowy height. Her features might have been sculpted by a master's hand. High cheekbones, aristocratic nose, green eyes framed by thick lashes, a wide mouth glistening with gloss in a dark shade of red that matched her nails.

She wore her hair up and anchored atop her head with ebony sticks in the Chinese style. Her dress was Chinese, too, a tightly fitting *cheongsam* in emerald silk, with a high mandarin collar, intricately knotted fasteners and side slits for ease of movement.

Tradition ended there, however. Where most *cheongsams* were slit to the knee, this one hiked high enough to display a length of smooth white thigh when she rose to greet her visitors.

"Mr. and Mrs. Callahan?"

Her voice was low and throaty, with only a trace of England left in it after so many years in the East.

"Welcome to Wang and Company."

She came forward, her hand outstretched. Jilly took it first and had to contain a start of surprise at the tight, almost knuckle-crunching grip.

The widow loosened her hold and turned to Hawk,

but he made no move to take her hand. Instead, he stared down at the woman with an expression Jilly couldn't interpret.

Neither could the widow, evidently. Chin tilting, she regarded him with a question in those forest-green eyes.

"Mr. Callahan?"

"I'm sorry." He gave his head a little shake and folded her hand in his. "It's just… Your perfume… It reminded me of someone I used to know."

Jilly took a surreptitious sniff and caught the barest hint of some exotic blend. Jasmine, she thought, and rose, mixed with dark, erotic musk.

Hall slipped her hand free of his and put it to the collar of her dress. Her eyes held Hawk's as she treated him to a cool smile.

"It's called Pandora. I have it imported from the south of France." Her long, red-tipped fingers fluttered at her throat. "You'll excuse me, I hope, if I say your friend has exquisite taste."

When Hawk gave a noncommittal nod, she gestured toward the sofa and chairs grouped near a glass wall with a panoramic view of the Kowloon side of the harbor.

"Would you care for a spot of tea? Or coffee? Or perhaps something stronger?"

"I would love a cup of tea," Jilly answered. "My husband prefers coffee."

She got it out this time without a stutter or stumble. Proud of herself, Gillian settled into a chair angled for maximum view. Hawk took the chair next to her.

After pressing the intercom to place the order with her assistant, Hall seated herself comfortably and crossed her legs with a whisper of silky nylon. "I read the e-mail you sent Mr. Wang. Although I tend to shy away from a direct role in our joint venture, I do occasionally work with clients."

She steepled her fingers and rested her chin on the bloodred tips.

"Now that I've met you, I think… Yes, I know I would enjoy helping you locate the treasures you hope to buy in Hong Kong. For a fee, of course."

"Which is?" Hawk inquired.

"Our standard finder's fee is fifteen percent. That could increase depending on the rarity of the items you're looking for and the time we spend finding them. What do you have in mind?"

Hawk deflected the question. "Before we get into specifics, I want to be sure your people can handle the packing and crating necessary to protect our purchases. We've had some problems in that area in the past."

"I assure you, we've shipped the most fragile items imaginable all over the world."

"Nevertheless, I'd need to see that side of your operation."

"Very well. Our warehouse is in Sheung Wan, the old part of the city." She glanced at her thin gold watch. "We could go this afternoon, but most of our workers will have left by the time we fight the traffic. It would be better if we went tomorrow morning."

"That works for us."

"Shall we say ten o'clock? I'll have a driver pick you up at your hotel. I believe you said you're putting up at the Peninsula?"

"We are," Hawk confirmed. "No need to send a car. We'll use one of the hotel's fleet."

"Very well. I'll have my secretary write out the address for you. Ah, here's our tea."

As Adriana poured hot water onto the fragrant tea leaves, excitement pulsed through her in fierce, feral waves. Her hand didn't shake, but only because she exercised every ounce of the unbreakable will that had kept her alive despite all odds.

She'd waited so long for this moment. Had planned it with such meticulous detail. Now he was here. The man she'd once loved and now hated with every thread of her being.

He didn't recognize her. How could he after so many fists to the face, so many broken bones? When she'd finally escaped, the surgeon who patched her together had botched the job so badly she hadn't recognized herself.

It had taken three bouts of cosmetic surgery to create the creature she now was. Different face. Different figure after all those months of near starvation. Very different voice, thanks to the bullet that had pierced her larynx.

Through all the years, all the pain, she'd survived the darkest, most horrific nights by retreating deep into herself. And by repeating a silent vow, over and over again.

They'd pay. Charlie Duncan. Mike Callahan. They'd pay for abandoning her to the bastard who'd raped and tortured her. They'd pay dearly.

She could still see Charlie's astonished face when she'd revealed her true identity. Still feel the hot blood that gushed down her arm when she'd slit his throat.

Now Mike had walked into her web.

The thrill of it, the savage delight of it, was an incandescent fire in her belly. She reveled in the scorching heat as she lifted her head and gave the woman playing his wife a cool smile.

"Milk or lemon, Mrs. Callahan?"

Chapter 5

"Hawk?"

The clink of silverware and crystal almost drowned the murmured query. Jilly crossed her elbows on the snowy linen tablecloth and leaned forward. Across the flickering candle, Hawk's face was a study in light and shadow.

The sight of him there, so strong, so solid—and so remote—started a strange ache in her chest. She felt left out. Or rather, left behind. Wherever he'd gone, she couldn't follow.

"Hawk?" she said again, louder this time.

His gaze shifted from a spot just over her shoulder.

"What?"

"You've barely touched your dinner, and I finished mine ten minutes ago. Shall we skip dessert and have coffee up in the room? That way you can tell me whatever it is that's bugging you."

He nodded and signaled for the waiter. They'd opted for an early dinner in one of the Peninsula's restaurants, as Jilly was starting to feel the cumulative effects of the long flight and busy day. Hawk had seemed to take both in stride…until that odd moment in Adriana Hall's office.

She thought about that as the elevator glided upward and about the woman herself. Hall was so gorgeous, so perfect.

Too perfect. She'd had some work done. Jilly took that as a given. The woman seemed young yet for nips and tucks, but then appointments with a cosmetic surgeon were now as common as visits to the hair salon.

"Here we are."

Hawk keyed the entry to their suite. When they entered, he reached into his suit coat pocket for the handheld scanner disguised as an iPod. A click of the wheel chirped out a report from the sensors he'd placed earlier.

"Key card entry, door one, nineteen hundred hours, six minutes. Key card entry, door one, twenty hundred hours, nine minutes."

Jilly made the mental calculation. "That's us. 8:09 p.m. The earlier entry was probably housekeeping. I see the bed is turned down."

One bed. Only one.

Housekeeping had jumped to the logical conclusion, given that their clothes hung side by side and their toiletries cluttered a single bedroom with its private bath.

The sight of that turned-down bed vaporized Jilly's weariness on the spot. A tingling sense of anticipation replaced it. The sensation sizzled along her nerves as Hawk pocketed the scanner.

"All clear?"

"Not yet."

Refusing to rely solely on technology, Hawk insisted on a physical sweep. Jilly watched and learned as he checked both bedroom suites and the luggage storage room before returning to the living area.

The dining room passed scrutiny, but he came to a sudden stop in the middle of the living room. His shoulders went taut, his eyes narrow.

"What is it?" Jilly asked, tensing.

"The ginger jar. It's been moved."

She followed his intent stare to one of the Chinese chests flanking the fireplace. A tall, lidded jar sat atop it. With its delicate, blue-and-white willow pattern, it matched the jar on the other side of the fireplace. Both jars sat dead center on their respective chests.

"It doesn't look to me like it's been moved."

"I pushed it a few inches to the left before we left this afternoon. Someone's moved it back."

The tension she'd picked up from him eased. "It must have been housekeeping. You can't mess with *feng shui.*"

She could tell from his impatient look that he wasn't into New Age decorating. Only the concept wasn't new in China. It went back thousands of years.

"*Feng shui,*" she repeated. "The phrase translates literally to wind and water. It has to do with striving for harmony with the forces of nature. That urge once governed everything from how a peasant plowed his field to the direction a woman faced while crouched on the birthing stool. Since *feng shui* also involved magic, sorcery and geomancy, it's been banned in modern China. The concepts of spatial and visual harmony are imbued in the culture, however."

Hawk still wasn't convinced. Jilly thought about reminding him that he was on her turf now. He should trust her on this. Instead, she shrugged out of her jacket and kicked off her shoes. Sinking into the plush sofa, she curled her feet under her.

"The idea of achieving a balance with nature isn't unique to China. The Greeks and Romans sacrificed to the gods of earth and sky. Ancient pagans believed spirits inhabited trees and boulders. They conducted all sorts of rituals designed to let them live in concert with their surroundings. Our so-called experts on global warming are dealing with exactly the same issue today."

"We're talking ginger jars here, not melting ice caps."

"Same problem, different scale. And speaking of global warming, I see the ice has melted in the champagne bucket. Why don't we pop the cork and finish off the strawberries for dessert?"

"Sounds good. You get the strawberries, I'll do the honors with the champagne."

The silver tray was dewy and cold to the touch. Jilly swiped the bottom with a napkin before positioning it within easy reach on the black lacquer coffee table. She snuck a berry and curled up on the sofa again while Hawk worked the foil cap off the cork.

He'd shed his Armani sport coat and rolled up the cuffs of his blue shirt. Jilly couldn't imagine how it had come through the long flight wrinkleless. The wizards in Field Dress, she mused as her appreciative gaze roamed the muscled chest and shoulders covered by the blue cotton blend.

When he untwisted the wire on the cap, the glint of gold on his wrist reminded her of unfinished business.

"We haven't called Control to give them an update on the mysterious Mrs. Hall."

Hawk was already busy with the champagne. "Go ahead and call in."

"Me?"

He frowned at her over the silver bucket. "Mac said she checked you out on your comm device."

"She did, she did! It's just… This is my first transmission from the field."

His mouth relaxed into a grin that said clearly every secret agent had to pop her cherry sometime.

"Go for it."

She lifted the pendant, held it out as far as the chain would allow and pressed Fu's root symbol. "This is Jade. Come in, Control."

She waited a few beats, straining to hear whatever came through the device's microdot speaker, before she remembered she had to press twice to receive.

"…and clear, Jade." Griff's laid-back Texas drawl came through with right-next-door clarity. "Ace here. What can I do for you?"

"Hawk and I wanted to know if you've dug up any more on Adriana Hall."

"Not yet. The lady's real savvy 'bout guarding her privacy. If we get her to squeak, I'll let you know."

"Okay. Or should I say 'roger'?"

"Most of us tend toward 'roger that,' sweet thing."

She could hear the laughter in his voice. Grinning, Jilly pressed the root again. "Roger that, stud. Now how do I terminate this transmission?"

"The usual phrase is over and…"

He broke off at the sound of a loud pop and came back with a sharp, "Jade?"

"It's okay. Hawk just opened a bottle of champagne."

"Did you say Hawk opened a bottle of bubbly? *Our* Hawk? Ole Deadeye himself? Well, well."

She lifted her gaze and caught ole Deadeye smiling and shaking his head.

"Y'all be sure to down a glass for us poor slobs in the trenches."

"We will," Hawk retorted. "Now clear the airways and get the hell back to work."

"Aye, aye, skipper. Over and out."

The pendant dropped back to the swell of Jilly's breasts. The jade bezel had warmed in her hand. She felt its heat through the silk of her blouse.

She could feel Hawk's warmth, as well, when he passed her a crystal flute and joined her on the sofa. His thigh nudging hers, he lifted his glass.

"To your first transmission."

"My first transmission, with many more to come."

His noncommittal grunt took some of the fizz from her sip of champagne.

"Still not happy about me going pro?"

"No."

"Hey, don't sugarcoat it on my account. I'm a big girl. I can take it straight."

His eyes locked with hers. "That's the only way I give it."

"Then tell me this. You went into the field with Diamond when she was a rookie. You trained Rogue from day one. Why are you so opposed to doing the same with me?"

"Diamond may look like a supermodel, but she's as tough as her code name. Same with Rogue. You…"

Jilly scrunched around and balanced her glass on the back of the sofa. "Me, what?"

"You're different."

"Not good enough, Hawk. You taught me to handle everything from a snub-nosed .38 to a 12 bore, double-barreled Thomas Turner. You've seen what I can do. You know I don't rattle or lose my cool when things go boom."

"You don't rattle or lose your cool on the firing range or at a trap shoot. They're a world away from the streets and sewers that spawn the kind of garbage we run up against."

He tipped his glass and downed a swallow, his eyes never leaving hers.

"The same streets and sewers spawned me, Gillian-with-a-J. When I fight, I fight dirty. In ways a girl with a lifetime membership to the Rock Springs Golf and Country Club could never stomach."

His reverse snobbery raised her hackles, but it was that "girl" that made her see red.

"So that's it."

Uncurling, she snapped her champagne glass down on the black lacquer coffee table. She didn't unleash her temper often, but when she did, her younger sister and brother knew to clear out. It was time—past time!—Hawk opened his eyes and saw her as she was, not as he wanted to see her.

"First, I stopped being a girl some years ago. Second, the fact that I play an occasional round of golf or tennis at my folks' club doesn't mean I can't handle whatever crawls out of a sewer. And that…" she stabbed her forefinger into his chest "…includes you, Michael Callahan."

"Jesus, Jilly."

"That's the problem in a nutshell. I'm still sweet little Jilly in your eyes."

In her own, too, she realized. Well, that would end, here and now.

"No more Jilly, Hawk. I'm Gillian. Or Jade. Got that? Jade."

She pushed up onto her knees. The abrupt movement tumbled her hair forward, onto her forehead. She tossed it back impatiently.

"Say it, Hawk. Jade."

"For God's sake."

"Say it!" She gave his chest another hard poke. "Jade!"

Cursing, he caught her hand and forced it down. Anger overrode her common sense at that point.

"All right." She twisted free of his hold. "Maybe this will convince you."

Bunching her fists in his shirtfront, she swooped in. The heat, the anger, fused her lips to his for the first second or two. When he remained rigid and unresponsive, sheer stubbornness took over. She altered her angle of attack and moved her mouth over his.

"How do you like it, Hawk? With teeth?"

She nipped at his lip, scraping the warm flesh.

"With tongue?"

Her hands slid over his shoulders, locked behind his neck. Her tongue taunted his.

His low growl triggered a memory of her mother's warning not to push him too hard or too far. A distant corner of her mind screeched at her to stop. Now. She'd made her point. In spades.

But she was beyond caution, beyond caring. What had begun in anger had stirred a fury of a different sort. The taste of him, the feel of him consumed her. Hunger stormed through her. Like a tsunami, it roared in her ears and swept everything away in its path except the violent need to feel his naked flesh. With her mouth locked on his, she dropped a hand again and tore at his shirt buttons.

A heartbeat later, she was flat on her back.

He straddled her, pinning her to the cushions. His fists banded her wrists and yanked her arms up. Those hazel eyes were merciless.

"You play with fire, *Jade,* you're apt to get burned."

She should have felt a flicker of fear. A few days ago she would have. Yesterday even, she might have cried uncle at this point and shied away from the ferocity in his eyes.

Now, everything in her exulted in the fact that she'd finally crashed through the wall. Her reply was low and throaty, her smile an invitation.

"So burn me, Hawk."

His grip tightened. His eyes darkened. He hovered

over her for two seconds. Three. Then his weight came down and he took what she was offering.

She strained upward, matching his fury. This was what she'd wanted from him. This was what she'd demanded from him. Raw hunger. Unthinking response.

Lost in the storm, she didn't realize he'd released her wrists until he raked a hand through her hair to anchor her head. His other hand thrust under her hip.

One tug, and he had her repositioned on the cushions. His knee pushed between hers, forcing them apart. A hard thigh pressed against the juncture of her thighs. Liquid heat shot from her belly to her breasts.

"Hawk," she gasped, trying to wedge her hands between them. She was desperate to get at his shirt again, in a frenzy to rip it open and plane *her* palms over his naked chest.

"You're crushing me," she panted. "Shift to the side. A little. Please."

He went still. Absolutely still. Then he muttered a vicious curse and shoved upright.

"I'm sorry. Jilly. Sweetheart. I'm sorry."

Oh, God! He'd completely misinterpreted her breathless plea. Groaning, she scrambled up and reached for him again.

"I'm not little Jilly anymore, Hawk. I'm Gillian, remember? Or Jade."

He frustrated her attempt to reconnect by simple expedient of getting to his feet.

"Okay. All right. Message received. I've had my head up my ass the past few years. I missed the transformation. Or maybe I just didn't want to see it."

The fury had died, but enough of the fire still burned for her to press him. "Now that your eyes are open, what do you see?"

His gaze dropped to her mouth, lifted again.

"I see trouble."

"Huh! Give me a minute to decide whether to feel flattered or insulted."

"What you should feel is relieved."

He raked a hand through his hair. It had lost its sophisticated, slicked-back look. So had Hawk. That almost made up for the wall he erected once again.

"The blinders are off, Jill…Gillian. I won't make the mistake of underestimating you again. But this isn't the time for either of us to open Pandora's box."

Pandora. The name conjured up a subtle blend of floral and musk. It also brought forcefully to mind the woman who ordered the scent from the south of France. As Hawk had known damned well it would.

"Okay," she conceded, blowing out a long breath. "*Your* message has been received. We need to shelve whatever this is between us and refocus on the mission."

"Yeah, we do. Starting now."

Was that regret in his eyes? It came and went so fast she couldn't be sure. But when he turned and went to the desk, he was all brisk business.

"I'm going to boot up the laptop. I want to pinpoint the location of Wang and Company's warehouse. I like to know before I go in how to get out."

"Need some help?"

"No."

Message received. Again. He wanted time and space

to let the last of the embers die. Her lips still throbbing from their tussle on the sofa, Gillian surrendered the field.

"I'm exhausted. I'll hit the shower and then go to bed."

An hour later the champagne bottle tilted in its bucket of lukewarm water. Hawk's flute sat untouched beside his laptop.

The shower had cut on about the time he'd pulled up a map of Sheung Wan district. It cut off while he was studying the maze of narrow, winding streets and alleys that climbed from the harbor to halfway up Victoria Peak's steep slopes.

He'd kept his eyes glued to the screen and forced himself to work possible escape routes. Despite his attempt at total concentration, he'd picked up the unmistakable swish of the duvet being pulled back. That was followed by the thump of a fist pummeling a pillow into shape.

Hawk was still at the computer when the bedroom light clicked off. Even then, he didn't relax. Jilly— Gillian—*Jade!*—had wound him so tight it would be next April or May before he worked out the kinks.

Utter silence blanketed the suite when Hawk finally rose and shoved aside the drapes. Any other time, Hong Kong's incredible nightscape would have drawn an admiring whistle. Tonight, he barely noticed the long wavy ribbon of lighted skyscrapers reflected in the waters of the bay.

He couldn't get Jilly—Jade, damn it!—out of his head. The taste of her. The feel of her. The jump she'd made from girl to woman to sensual, seductive female.

He hadn't been totally truthful with her earlier. He hadn't had his head *all* the way up his ass. He'd noticed the changes. Hell, he'd have to have been blind not to. He'd simply refused to acknowledge them.

Just as he'd refused to admit she had the smarts and the skills to survive in this dirty business. His every instinct made him want to protect her, shield her. Keep her from being gunned down and choking on her own blood.

He gripped both hands on the terrace railing. Eyes unseeing, he stared at the lights across the harbor.

That's how Diane had died. Choking. Gurgling. Sobbing for him, for Charlie, for *someone* to help her.

Hawk had heard her. Despite the roar of the chopper hovering above the canopy. Despite Charlie's frantic shouts that they had to get out of there. Despite the bullets splatting through the vines and the searing agony of Hawk's shattered leg.

He'd heard her and staggered to his feet.

Blood from a head wound poured into his eyes, blinding him. He tripped over a root. He went down again, his injured leg ablaze with pain.

The breeze carried harbor scents. Fish. Diesel. But all Hawk could smell was damp earth and rotting vegetation.

Diane! Hold on!

He'd rolled onto his good side.

Dug his fingers into the spongy ground.

I'm coming! I'm coming!

The cries stopped before he'd crawled five yards. The choking continued for another second, maybe two. Then Charlie was shouting and dragging on his arm.

She's dead, Mike. She's dead.

The hell she is!
She's dead! We gotta get on the chopper.
No!

Snarling, Mike threw off his grip and tried to get his good leg under him.

That's when Charlie clipped him. A swift, bruising fist to the jaw. With his vision a blurred curtain of red, Mike didn't see it coming. He went down, landing on his shattered leg once more, and the world exploded into darkness.

He woke two days later to the mingled scents of starched sheets and antiseptic. But even now, even after all these years, he carried the stink of that damp, decaying vegetation inside him.

That, and the distant memory of the perfume Diane always wore.

Chapter 6

Gillian woke to a haze of diffused sunlight and the tantalizing scent of fresh brewed coffee. Knuckling the sleep from her eyes, she rolled over and propped herself up on an elbow.

Hawk had slept beside her last night. The pillow on the far side of the bed was indented, the covers rumpled. By contrast, the space between them yawned wide and undisturbed.

Some honeymoon.

Huffing, she flopped back down on the Peninsula's luxurious sheets. She couldn't help imagining how different last night might have been. She'd certainly stirred the proverbial sleeping tiger. Even now, her skin flushed at the memory of his mouth rough and hard on hers, his hand mounding the tender flesh of her breast.

If only she'd kept her mouth shut! So Hawk's weight had crushed her in the sofa cushions? Telling him so had produced exactly the wrong result. He hadn't just shifted his weight, he'd removed it entirely. Then he'd gone all guilty and remorseful on her.

Not her. Jilly.

With a grimace, she threw off the covers and padded into the bathroom. The black lace negligee Field Dress had procured whispered against her skin as she planted both hands on the marble vanity.

"Do *not* forget," she instructed the tangle-haired female in the mirror. "You declared your independence from little Jilly last night. There will be no regressing."

She looked her alter ego square in the eye.

"You're Jade. Hard-nosed undercover operative. Cool. Confident. Totally and completely focused on the mission. Now get your butt in gear."

Twenty minutes later, she strolled into the living room. She'd dressed casually but elegantly in the Bruno Magli ankle boots, black wool slacks and a cashmere sweater set in cobalt. The sweaters complimented the sapphires in her ring and gave the stones a deeper hue. Her jade charm dangled from its gold chain.

Hawk was at the dining table, a silver tea and coffee service at his elbow. He, too, had opted for casual. Gray slacks, a fawn-colored turtleneck and a navy blazer. The blazer's breast pocket sported the embroidered patch of the American Marksmanship Association.

Despite her stern lecture in the bathroom, the mere sight of the man triggered all sorts of inappropriate thoughts. Most of them centered around what it would be like to face him across a breakfast table if they'd finished what they'd started last night.

She pinned on her best cool, confident secret-agent smile. "Good morning."

His eyes met hers over the coffeepot. "'Morning."

Well, thank goodness! She wasn't the only one dogged by thoughts of what did—and didn't—happen on that sofa. The wariness was evident in his carefully neutral greeting.

"I wasn't sure what you usually have for breakfast, so I waited to order from room service. Or would you prefer to go down to one of the restaurants?"

So polite. So deliberate.

"Room service works for me. Just toast," she said when he lifted one of the cordless phones conveniently scattered throughout the suite. "Wheat, not white, with plum preserves."

He added a full English breakfast to her order while she looked over the assortment of teas on the silver tray. White Willow, she decided, anticipating its delicate kick. While the tea steeped, she settled into the chair beside Hawk.

"Is that the map you pulled up last night?"

Nodding, he angled the printed sheet in her direction. "I don't think we'll have much problem with an escape route if we need one. Not in this maze."

Maze understated the case by exponential degrees. The map detailed the wharves edging the waterfront of Hong Kong Island, directly across Victoria Harbour from Kowloon. Wide boulevards and the skyscrapers of the business district fronted the wharves. Jammed in behind the skyscrapers was the area known as the Mid-levels, so named because it climbed and twisted and clung halfway up the steep slopes of mountains dominating the island.

Streets, such as they were, tripped all over themselves. Some doubled back to where they started. Others wound in seemingly endless circles. Gillian had heard varying estimates of how many million people lived and worked, loved and played, were born and died, in the teeming Mid-levels. The correct number was probably lost in the mists that rolled down from the Peak on rainy days.

"I take it this is Wang and Company's warehouse?"

Hawk had marked the building with a red *X*. It was in the heart of Sheung Wan, close to the wharves.

"Good location," she commented. "Very handy for moving containers of antiques to the dock for transport to the main container facility."

The Ching Mai Container Facility was a huge, sprawling complex. Gillian had caught a glimpse of it when they'd landed yesterday. Thousands upon thousands of containers the size of railroad cars had been lined up in rows, waiting to be loaded onto ships.

"Do you think the infected monkeys could have been stuffed into a shipping container at the main port facility?"

"It's possible," Hawk replied. "Smugglers working the black-market animal trade could easily have cohorts among the dockworkers."

"What's security like at those complexes?"

"Tight, given the terrorist threat these days. Very

tight. But where there's a will—and enough money changing hands—there will always be a way. Case in point, the eleven Nigerian refugees who were found dead at the Port of Miami last year. Immigration officials estimate the temperatures inside the container they were locked in topped a hundred and thirty degrees."

Gillian couldn't have worked for the State Department without hearing reports of the flourishing human smuggling trade. Young Thai girls, especially, had been victimized in recent years. The thought of any living creature being locked into a dark, unventilated container and shipped halfway around the world made her really, really want to nail some of the bastards engaged in the despicable trade.

"Based on what you learned from the raid on the Vhrana temple," Hawk said, frowning down at the map, "we know at least one endangered gibbon arrived in the States in a container leased by Wang and Company. We start there. See how they package the items they ship. Talk to their warehouse manager. Go through the facade of purchasing several items for shipment. If nothing pops there, we'll track the items to the container facility."

Gulping, Gillian flashed again on those thousands of metal containers lined up at the Ching Mai facility. She was still dealing with the possibility of having to trudge through endless rows when their breakfast arrived.

Gillian noticed the odd tingle while spreading plum jam over a slice of toast. A second later, she gasped and dropped her knife.

"Oh!"

Hawk's head whipped around. With a shamefaced grin, she set the toast on her plate and reached for her Fu.

"Sorry. I wasn't expecting... The warmth... Er, incoming."

He didn't actually roll his eyes, but he wanted to. She could see it in his face as she fumbled with the charm.

"This is Jade. Come in, Control."

"Mornin', sweet thing."

Griff's lazy drawl drifted through the microdot speaker.

"Morning, Ace."

"You and ole Deadeye nursin' sore heads from too much champagne?"

"Nope."

"That's 'negative' in spook talk, darlin'."

"Okay, negative. What's up?"

His teasing tone faded. "Hawk there with you?"

"Right here," he answered.

"I finally turned over some info on Wang and Company. Turns out, there is no Wang. Or any company, for that matter. It's a dummy holding account, a front for a corporation called Pan-Dor, Associated."

Gillian's gaze flew to Hawk's. "Did you say Pan-Dor?" she asked.

"Roger that. The corporation is owned by a shadowy entity I haven't been able to pin down. The attorneys who set it up must have received their legal training from the mafioso. I've hit so many blinds and double-blinds, they're making me dizzy. But I'll press until I put a face or faces to the name."

"I think we already have one," Hawk said. "Adriana Hall. She let drop yesterday that she orders a special perfume from the south of France. It's called Pandora."

"Coincidence?"

"Could be. Then again…"

"Yeah, I know. Coincidences can get you real dead, real fast, in this business. If Adriana Hall *is* Pan-Dor, Associated, the lady has a thing for keeping her business dealings private."

"So it seems. We're meeting with her again this morning. We'll let you know how it goes."

"Roger that."

Hawk reset his iPod-like intrusion-detection system before they left the suite. Gillian waited in the foyer with her purse slung over her shoulder, while he physically rechecked the alignment of the items in the dresser drawer and positioned his laptop and the desk notepad at precise angles. That done, he eyed the blue-and-white ginger jars atop their black lacquer chests.

Common sense said Gillian was right. If he moved one of the things, housekeeping would probably do the *feng shui* thing and recenter it. He started for the foyer, took three steps, and stopped.

With all those little drawers and top-lifting lids, the lacquer chests provided too tempting a target. Anyone conducting a search of the room wouldn't pass them by. Neither could Hawk. He strode back and nudged one of the ginger jars to the right.

"I know," he said to a plainly amused Gillian. "Some habits just go too deep to jettison."

* * *

Some memories, too.

Hawk's vectored in with savage velocity when Adriana Hall came forward to greet them at the entrance to her storage and shipping facility.

It was the perfume. That damned perfume. The scent crawled all over his nerves.

"Good morning, Mr. and Mrs. Callahan."

She was wearing a Chinese dress again this morning. Scarlet silk, this time, embroidered with gold. The male in Hawk couldn't fail to notice how the high-collared outfit clung to her slender curves. Or how the side slits swished open when she walked.

"I trust you slept well after your long flight?"

"Very well, thank you."

He didn't contradict Gillian's polite reply, but sleep had been the last thing on his mind last night. He'd finally made it to the bedroom just before dawn. Even then he'd dozed only in snatches.

Some of his sleeplessness he could blame on the raw memories of his last mission with Special Ops. Most of it, however, was the direct result of the hunger Gillian had unleashed. He still couldn't believe how close he'd come to taking what she'd offered. Her angry attempt to make him see her as woman had short-circuited every one of the systems he'd put in place to keep from doing just that.

He knew now he'd *wanted* to think of her as Jilly. *Wanted* to nourish an avuncular relationship between them. In fact, he'd worked damned hard to maintain his role as an old family friend. He'd been comfortable with that role. Most of the time.

He'd felt himself slipping on occasion. Like when she would grin and invite him to share some private joke. Or when those melting blue eyes would widen with assumed innocence, a sure sign she was about to say or do something outrageous. Or that time she'd swung around in her chair and her skirt had hiked up. Hawk couldn't walk straight afterward. Adriana Hall gave Gillian Ridgeway zero competition in the leg department.

Or any other. Remembering how she'd moved under him last night made sweat pool at the base of Hawk's spine.

"Are you a sharpshooter, Mr. Callahan?"

He wrenched his mind from the vision of Gillian stretched out and panting on the sofa and found Adriana Hall studying the patch on his blazer pocket. With its rifles crossed over a bullseye, the embroidered insignia held her intent gaze.

"He's one of the world's best," Gillian bragged with wifely pride. "My husband has won medals at every international competition on the books."

"Is that so?" Those green eyes lifted to Hawk's face. "Do you shoot trap? Skeet? Paper targets?"

"Whatever is in my sights."

"Indeed? How interesting. Would you care for tea before I show you around?"

Gillian answered for them again. "We're fine, thanks." Playing to her role, she tucked her arm in Hawk's. The diamonds and sapphires on her left hand winked in the sunlight. "We slept in and had a late breakfast this morning."

"Very well," Hall said coolly. "You mentioned that

you wanted to see our packing and crating operation. Please, come with me."

She led the way up a short flight of steps to a concrete loading dock. Two metal shipping containers sat on the dock. One was closed. The other was open and half-filled with wooden crates. Hawk made a mental note of the address stenciled on the crates before dropping a casual inquiry.

"Any chance Mr. Wang will join us?"

Hall halted and turned to face them. Chin tipped, she regarded Hawk through the screen of her lashes.

"There is no Mr. Wang...as I suspect you may have already discovered."

"I did some digging after our meeting yesterday," he acknowledged. "Care to tell me why my wife and I should do business with someone who hides her true identity?"

"Ah, yes. My true identity."

There was no mistaking the expression in her cat's eyes now. The amusement had an edge to it, though, as did her retort.

"Which identity would you prefer, Mr. Callahan? I have several. Bubble-headed blonde. Helpless female. Bereaved widow, still struggling to cope with the death of her lord and master. None of those personas inspire confidence in buyers intending to outlay rather large sums on money on the treasures I acquire for them. Hence the fictitious Mr. Wang."

"What skin are you wearing today?" Gillian inquired politely. "Or did you slither into a new one for us?"

That drew a swift, narrow-eyed stare from Hall and a warning squeeze of her arm from Hawk.

"I'm sorry," she said with a bland smile that implied the opposite. "I didn't mean to sound rude. But as you indicate, we intend to spend a large amount of cash. We want to know who, exactly, we're dealing with."

"You're dealing with the real me, Mrs. Callahan." Her gaze shifted to Hawk. "Complete and unadorned."

Unadorned, hell!

Gillian managed to swallow her response to that ridiculous statement. The effort almost choked her. She did *not* like this woman. She liked even less the way Adriana Hall ate Hawk with her eyes.

Bitch.

"Please tell me, Mr. Callahan. Do we proceed now that you know I am Wang and Company?"

The woman was determined to cut Gillian out of the conversation. *Double bitch.*

Hawk didn't let her get away with it. "What do you think, sweetheart? Do we proceed?"

"Well…" Sweetheart pretended to ponder the question. "Since we're here, I guess we should let Ms. Hall show us her operation."

"Why don't you call me Adriana?"

Why don't you kiss my ass?

"Certainly. And I'm Gillian."

That produced a regal nod and another glance in Hawk's direction.

"Mike," he said.

"Mike," she echoed, her eyes all over him again.

Gillian identified the emotion that slashed into her without the least difficulty. Jealousy, pure and simple. Yielding to it, she kept Hawk's arm tucked tight against her side throughout their tour of Wang and Company's packaging and crating operation.

It resembled many similar operations she'd observed in Beijing and its environs. The facilities were basic at best. Concrete floors. No heat or air-conditioning. Long, wooden workbenches positioned under strings of naked lightbulbs.

A crew of six women sat at one bench, wielding bubble wrap and padded brown paper with careful efficiency. Gillian's appreciative eye roamed the objects they were preparing for shipment. The treasures included cloisonné vases, Tang dynasty bronzes and exquisite terracotta statues that might have come from an emperor's tomb.

One piece in particular snagged her attention. The small ceramic altar sat by itself at the end of the workbench. It was about a foot long and six inches high. Several small drinking vessels and plates in different shapes sat atop the altar. To be used for offering food and libations to departed ancestors, Gillian knew.

Her breath catching, she dragged Hawk toward the end of the bench. "This looks like a Ming dynasty altar table!"

Looked like, but wasn't.

She recognized it for a fake the moment she bent for a closer inspection. The chop incised in one leg of the table used present-day rather than twelfth-century symbols. Before she could voice her disappointment, Adriana Hall stroked a hand over the ceramic glaze.

"I procured this altar for an Australian buyer, but he balked at the price. If it interests you, I might be willing to come down a bit."

Recalled to her role as a determined buyer, Gillian feigned a collector's greed. "To what?"

"Shall we say five thousand?"

"Dollars or pounds?"

"Pounds."

Triple bitch.

"We'll take it."

"Whoa!" Hawk's protest held a ring of genuine husbandly alarm. "Shouldn't we discuss this first?"

"Oh, dear. I keep forgetting."

The pouty smile Gillian turned on Hall was as phony as the one the woman had turned on her earlier.

"I now have to answer to a lord and master. That *is* how you phrased it, isn't it?"

Adriana had to work at masking her feelings as she moved away to give the couple privacy for their "discussion." Mike's pseudo wife was adding unexpected kick to the vengeance she'd waited so long to exact.

Callahan wasn't the only one who'd done some digging. Adriana had spent a good part of last night milking her sources. She knew all about Gillian Ridgeway. Her queries had yielded a wealth of information about the pampered daughter of one of Washington's power couples.

The woman would have to be eliminated. That was a given. Obviously, she was working with Callahan. Why else would she pretend a marriage Adriana could find no record of? Or disguise the knowledge she must have gained during her years at the American Embassy in Beijing? Ridgeway had recognized the altar table as a fake the moment she'd bent to examine the chop. Yet she'd played the eager collector to perfection, followed hard by the chagrined wife.

With a swift change of plans, Adriana decided to fleece the rich Mrs. Ridgeway out of every dollar she could before she had her body dumped into Victoria Harbour.

Chapter 7

"I don't like that woman."

Gillian plunked the bubble-wrapped altar onto the limo's seat and snapped on her seat belt.

"Aside from the fact she deals in reproductions instead of the genuine article, she…"

"What?" Hawk's startled glance dropped to the package nestled between them. "Are you saying you just wrote a four-figure check for a fake?"

She dismissed the money with an impatient wave. "Don't worry. I'll e-mail my bank and have them sit on the check until we determine whether Ms. Hall is as bogus as her merchandise. Although…"

Honesty compelled her to make a grudging concession.

"She didn't actually *say* it was genuine. Nor did she

offer to provide a certificate of authenticity. She just let her latest fish swim onto her hook."

And swim she had. Gillian had stuck to her role but had *not* enjoyed playing the fool for Adriana Hall.

"So what's your take?" she asked Hawk. "Did you pick up anything to indicate Hall is into the black-market animal trade as well as counterfeit antiques?"

She certainly hadn't, and God knew she'd looked into every corner and listened closely to the workers' chatter. She would love to pin a smuggling rap on the condescending blonde. To her intense disappointment, Hawk shook his head.

"Nothing popped for me, either. But I'm not taking Hall out of the picture yet. There's something about the woman… I can't quite get a fix on her."

Gillian could, and the fix wasn't pretty.

"Why don't we just ask her outright about the gibbons?"

"It may come to that," he replied, "but I'm not ready to tip our hand yet. We'll keep up the facade for a little while longer. Let her take us around to some of her sources, as she offered to do."

The prospect didn't particularly thrill Gillian. Adriana Hall had made it abundantly clear she considered Hawk's wife a minor player.

"Did you notice how she directed most of her comments to you? You'd think someone who disguised her true role in the company because of prejudices against women would be a little more sensitive in how she dealt with other women."

"You'd think," he agreed, his gaze fixed on something he'd spotted through the side window. "What the hell is that?"

She leaned around him and gave a yelp of delight.

"That, my friend, is the next best way to experience Hong Kong after a ride on the Star Ferry." A flick of a switch slid back the Plexiglas partition. "Stop the car," she told the driver. "We're getting out here."

"We've got work to do," Hawk protested. "We need to nail down the truck company that transports Hall's containers to the deep water port and…"

"We will, we will." She already had the door open. "After we take a ride on the Mid-levels Escalator."

Hawk got out beside her and craned his neck to look up. And up. And up.

"Jesus. How long is this thing?"

"Loooong. A half mile or more."

The covered, outdoor escalator looked like a metal caterpillar zigzagging from the central business district to the residential neighborhoods of the Mid-levels. Its twenty separate segments and moving sidewalks traveled downward during morning rush hour, then changed direction around ten-thirty. A quick glance at her watch confirmed Hong Kong's high-tech people-mover had made the switch.

"C'mon. We need to buy an Octopus card."

She hauled Hawk to a booth in the ultramodern base station to purchase the ticket that served as an instant credit card. Depending on how much the purchaser shelled out, the chip embedded in the card allowed him or her to purchase everything from public transportation to cell phones.

"And we think we're so advanced," Hawk muttered as he flashed his card at an optical scanner. Moments later, they joined the stream aiming for the first set of moving stairs.

"Walkers to the left, standers to the right," Gillian warned. "You'd better scoot over if you don't want to get mowed down."

He edged to the right on the step behind her and kept one hand on the rail. When she angled around to act as tour guide, she was nestled in the crook of his arm.

Hawk's mind had still been on shipping containers and trucking companies, but their closeness produced an instant reaction. He could feel his body harden as a sparkle lit her eyes.

"We've missed rush hour. That's when the ride is really fun. It's elbow-to-elbow, everyone in lockstep then. Right now, the crowd is mostly tourists and shoppers and school kids."

She loves this, Hawk realized. The hustle and bustle of humanity, the pulsing vitality and ageless mystery of the East. Most Westerners would feel out of place or nervous about trying to find their way through the jumble of streets. Gillian just dived right in.

"The trip up only takes about twenty minutes," she told him as they got off the first escalator and walked the few yards to the next. "But we'll travel a thousand years or more in terms of culture and tradition. From modern day Hong Kong..." Her sweeping gesture encompassed the skyscrapers and multistory condos of the lower district. "...to the shops and houses and temples of the old city."

When they traveled upward, Hawk began to see the transition she'd described. At the lower levels, down near the business district, the department stores' windows lining the moving stairs displayed designer labels and the eating and drinking establishments sported names like Starbucks and Josephine's.

Gradually these trendy department stores gave way to small shops displaying local produce, clothing and the inevitable electronics. Interspersed among the shops were noodle parlors and temples where worshippers could pause on their way to or from work to buy a stick of incense and say a quick prayer.

Apartment buildings crowded the shops. Mostly utilitarian buildings constructed of gray concrete. The higher up Gillian and Hawk went, the narrower the apartments got, until they appeared little more than one room wide. Satellite dishes were attached to a number of balconies. Others sported bamboo poles with washing speared through them to dry.

As the escalator carried them upward, Hawk caught glimpses of life inside those narrow apartments. TVs flickered in some. Family altars and red banners displaying Chinese characters in gold decorated the entrances to others.

"We're coming into the really old section now," Gillian advised when they reached the fifteenth section. "It's gradually being squeezed out by new construction above and below, but you can still get a feel for what life was like before electricity and satellite dishes."

Wooden shanties clung to the steep hills on either side of the escalator. They were piled one on top of the other in seemingly endless, tip-tilted layers. Dirt tracks cut between the layers. These narrow streets were alive with activity. Chickens, goats and the occasional pig rooted amid baskets of refuse waiting for collection. Women in straw hats and traditional Chinese dress squatted in the dirt, cooking or washing clothes in kettles. Children tossed balls or climbed hills. Old men in long coats shambled along.

Commerce was alive and well in this section of Hong Kong, too. Vendors waited at each of the escalator stops, selling cheap hats, postcards, pomegranates and tea steeped in brass kettles suspended on shoulder poles.

"*Shey-shey.*" Smiling and shaking her head, Gillian wove through the milling throng. "*Shey-shey.*"

"What are you saying to them?" Hawk asked as they headed for yet another section of the moving stairs.

"Thank you. Just keep repeating it politely and forge ahead."

"*Shey-shey. Shey-shey. Shey…*"

The fluted trill of a canary sounded just off to his side. Hawk glanced around and saw a familiar pair of pink sneakers topped by a tattered pink T-shirt.

"Isn't that the kid from the promenade?"

Gillian spied the girl at the same moment the pint-size con artist lifted her head and spotted them. Her eyes rounded in recognition, then flooded with fright.

"Ai-ah!"

Spinning, she tried to run, but the crowd and the wooden cage she clutched in one grubby fist impeded her way. Frustrated by the solid wall of humanity, she darted toward the down escalator.

"Hey, kid! It's okay! I'm not looking to recoup my twenty bucks."

Obviously, she didn't understand, but the shout produced another panicky glance over her shoulder. Hawk's heart stopped dead in his chest when the violent twist threw her off balance.

"Look out!"

A high wail tore from the girl's throat. Her small arms flailing, she teetered at the top of the steep metal stairs. Her scream was still ripping across the air when Hawk lunged through the startled bystanders.

He caught her just as she started to tumble downward and swung her, cage and all, into his arms. "It's okay. It's okay, baby. I've got you."

Her small body convulsing with fright, the girl locked her arms around his neck. Wrenching sobs replaced her terror-filled wails. The canary's agitated chirping added to the din assaulting Hawk's ears.

"Don't cry, kid. You're okay." He patted her heaving back and threw Gillian a pleading look. "I could use a little help here!"

Murmuring in Chinese, she stroked the girl's hair. The sobs lost some of their piercing volume, but the canary continued to chirp its fool head off.

When Gillian tried to relieve Hawk of his burden, the girl gave a muffled shriek, tightened her stranglehold and crawled up his chest to bury her face in his neck.

"Oh, for…!" He eyed the crowd that had gathered with a touch of desperation. "See if any of these folks know the kid. They could take her home."

Gillian's queries produced only head shakes and

murmured negatives. A sudden scuffle parted the crowd. The boy who pushed his way through stumbled to a stop when he saw Hawk, then gulped and charged forward.

"Why you hurt Mei Lin? She little. I take your money, not her."

He dug several wadded bills from the pocket of his jeans and shoved them at Hawk.

"Here. Take dollars. No hurt Mei Lin. No call police."

"I don't want your money, and I have no intention of calling the police. Mei Lin's not hurt, just scared. She tripped and almost fell down the escalator."

The kid queried his sister in urgent Chinese. She answered with watery sniffles and what Hawk assumed were affirmatives.

"Okay, sweetheart." Gently, he tried to disengage. "Your brother's here."

When the girl refused to budge, Hawk patted her back again and addressed the kid. "What's your name?"

"Young Tau."

"Tell your sister you'll take her home."

"No have home."

"You must eat and sleep somewhere."

"Sometimes in street." He made a vague gesture toward the shanties. "Sometimes with Ah Chang."

"Who's Ah Chang?"

"Honorable Grandfather."

The crowd had begun to disperse, but Mei Lin still wouldn't loosen her death grip.

"Am I being conned again?" Hawk asked Gillian.

"I'm not sure." Frowning, she shifted her gaze from the boy's Nikes to the girl's pink T-shirt. "The shoes look almost new, but the T-shirts are ragged, and the air is cool enough that they should be wearing jackets."

As if to underscore the observation, Mei Lin shivered and burrowed deeper into Hawk's warmth.

Well, hell! Cradling her against his chest, he glared at the boy. "Take us to this grandfather of yours."

Young Tau hesitated, clearly trying to decide whether to comply…or how he could milk the situation, Hawk thought sardonically.

"Now, kid!"

As slums went, these weren't the most miserable Hawk had ever seen. Central America and Mexico had worse. In some of the former Russian republics, whole families lived in abandoned railcars. The U.S., too, had its share of homeless sleeping on park benches or in cardboard boxes. Yet the sheer density of the population inhabiting this jumble of tile- and tin-roofed shacks made it unique in Hawk's experience.

With Mei Lin still cradled in his arms, he and Gillian dodged wet washing and picked their way carefully over uneven ruts. Dogs sniffed at their heels. A rooster hissed and fanned his tail feathers, guarding his harem of hens. The sharp tang of burning charcoal from cooking braziers mingled with dust and incense from ceramic altars almost identical to the one Gillian had just shelled out megabucks for.

People in all shapes and sizes added their stamp to the mix. Old men with drooping mustaches sucked on long-stemmed pipes and huddled over mah-jongg boards.

Women squatted beside the glowing braziers. Youngsters who should have been in school played in the dirt.

Despite the cool temperatures, several of the toddlers showed bare bottoms through cutouts in the seat of their pajamas or overalls. The utility of that became obvious when Hawk spotted a young girl holding her baby brother over a ditch to go to the bathroom.

"You come."

Young Tau crooked an imperious finger before ducking between two shacks that leaned so close together their corrugated tin roofs almost touched. Putting a hand to the back of Mei Lin's head to protect her from the sharp edges, Hawk held out his other hand to Gillian. They made it through the narrow gap with mere inches to spare.

"How far to your grandfather's?" he asked Young Tau.

"No far. There."

He poked a finger toward the jumble of shacks clinging to the ridge directly above them, reached by a rickety set of steps.

"Gillian, can you manage the stairs in those boots?"

"I'm okay. Can *you* manage Mei Lin and her canary?"

Hawk would have jettisoned the bird a ways back if he didn't now suspect it provided a primary source of income for the kids.

"I can manage. Hang on to my arm."

Young Tau scrambled up ahead of them and ducked under a weathered lintel that must have once been painted a bright red. Hawk was hauling Gillian up the last few feet when a stooped old man hobbled out. His ankle-length, quilted cotton gown hung loosely on his thin frame. The worn hem brushed the tops of his black slippers. Even from ten or fifteen yards away, Hawk could see the cataracts clouding his eyes. The pupils were almost as white as his long, wispy beard.

Huffing a little after the climb, Gillian greeted him in Chinese. He bowed deeply and answered at some length.

"Ah Chang thanks you for saving Mei Lin from a fall," she translated for Hawk. "He says he isn't really her grandfather, and Young Tau isn't her brother. They all sort of just adopted each other. He invites us to come in and take tea."

Hawk eyed the shanty with some misgiving. The front end was supported on stilts dug into the hillside at sharp angles. The rear section looked as though it had been carved out of the dirt.

Gillian had already stooped under the lintel, however, leaving him little choice but to set Mei Lin down and follow. Once inside he had to crouch to keep from banging his head against the poles that supported the roof or bumping into dust-coated lanterns decorated with faded red tassels.

"Honorable Grandfather say, Mister please to sit here." Young Tau patted a wooden chair with curved arms. "Madam, please to take cushion."

Since the chair looked to be the only substantial piece of furniture in the two-room dwelling, Hawk started to defer to the elderly gentleman. Gillian stilled him with a warning glance and sank onto her cushion.

"Honorable Grandfather does us much honor. We are pleased to sit."

Ah Chang hobbled to another cushion. When he sat, Hawk had to hide a wince at the audible creak of his joints.

Gillian made the introductions. "This is my husband, Callahan *Shen Sheung*."

"Cal Han *Shen Sheung,*" Young Tau echoed.

"Call-*a*-Han."

"Cal Han," the boy repeated.

"That's close enough. I am Gillian."

Her name was immediately shortened to Jill-An.

The introductions out of the way, the kids scrambled to brew fresh tea. They'd obviously performed the task many times before. Young Tau stirred the coals in a small brazier while little Mei Lin lifted a chipped porcelain teapot from a low shelf. From the reverent way she handled the piece, Hawk guessed it was reserved for special guests.

A murmur of polite Chinese drew his attention to Ah Chang. Gillian responded in the same lilting, sing-song dialect.

"Honorable Grandfather wishes to know why we visit Hong Kong. I told him we've come to buy antiques."

The old man stroked his beard and added another comment.

"He says we must be careful," she translated solemnly. "There are many fakes on the market."

"You don't say," Hawk drawled.

"He says that he has lived many years," she added after another colloquy. "He knows what is genuine and what is not. He offers his assistance, should we wish it. The children, too, are very knowledgeable of what happens on the streets."

Yeah, right. Hawk was still struggling with the fact that he was partnered with Gillian on this op. All he needed was to add a blind old man and a couple of junior grifters to his team.

Except…

Pretending to need their services might be a way to slip them a little extra income. God knew, they could use it. Hawk had only a restricted view of the other room, but from what he could see, it was even more sparsely furnished than this one.

"Please tell, er, Honorable Grandfather that we would be grateful for any assistance he wishes to provide. But only if he'll allow us to pay a commission on the pieces he authenticates."

The warm approval in Gillian's eyes went a long way to stilling some of Hawk's doubts about his team's unexpected expansion.

The man listened intently to the proposal and dipped his head in a nod.

"Done," Gillian said after another brief discussion. "Honorable Grandfather and the kids will take the ferry across the harbor tomorrow afternoon and meet us at the hotel to look over our potential purchases. I told him we would be honored to return his hospitality by taking them to dinner."

"That's fine. Better ask him, though, why the kids aren't in school. Isn't education mandatory throughout China?"

"It is, but some kids fall through the cracks here, just as they do at home. Mei Lin is probably still too young for school. Young Tau…"

"No time school," the boy answered for himself as he poured hot water into the porcelain teapot. "Very busy, work very hard."

Looking at the skinny kid with the jet-black hair, Hawk saw himself twenty-five or -six years ago. He'd been just as thin, just as hungry, but considerably more belligerent. Too bad he hadn't stumbled across an Honorable Grandfather to rein him in. Maybe he wouldn't have collected so many bruises or spent so many nights curled up in culverts.

He'd learned how to survive the hard way. He'd also picked up some interesting tidbits of information. So had Young Tau, he'd bet.

"Hey, kid. You know anything about animals being shipped out of Hong Kong illegally?"

The wary expression that dropped over the boy's face countered his quick negative.

"Know nothing."

"How about animal parts? Tigers' eyes or bear gall or…?"

"Young Tau see nothing, know nothing."

The denial was too quick, the glance he darted at the old man too furtive. Hawk didn't press the issue. Obviously Honorable Grandfather had drawn some lines regarding the kids' money-making ventures. Just as obviously, Young Tau knew more than he was willing to admit in front of the others. Hawk would have to get him alone and have a fistful of dollars handy.

A swish of sneakers on the dirt floor directed his attention to Mei Lin. With a shy smile and a murmur of Chinese, she offered him a thimble-size cup of steaming tea. Hawk accepted it and looked to Gillian for a translation.

"She says she thanks you for catching her before she fell. She thinks maybe you're not so big and ugly after all."

"Shey-shey," Hawk replied.

Mei Lin's rosebud mouth parted. A moment later, she burst into giggles. Young Tau snorted, and the old man raised a blue-veined hand to hide a gap-toothed smile.

"What did I say?"

"You got the tones wrong." Gillian's eyes were filled with laughter. "You just wished her a cold donkey."

Still giggling, the girl crawled into Hawk's lap and proceeded to chatter away. He didn't understand a word. He didn't have to. She didn't appear to require a response.

"Your husband very good to children," Ah Chang commented to Gillian.

"So it appears," she murmured.

Her heart turned over at the sight of Hawk's head bent attentively to Mei Lin's. She'd known him for so long, had watched him interact with both her younger sister and brother. A few moments in his company and shy, quiet Samantha would shed her natural reserve like an old coat. Even the irrepressible Tank was convinced the two of them were communicating man-to-man.

Yet until this moment, Gillian's main preoccupation with Mike Callahan had been sexual. First as a target of her teenaged crush, then as a challenge to her femininity. Only recently had she admitted to a hunger for him that grew more urgent by the hour.

Now…

Now, she realized with shattering insight, she wanted more. She wanted a future that included moments like this. A future where she and Hawk shared more than heat, indulged more than animal hunger.

"You have sons? Daughters?"

She dragged her attention from Hawk and Mei Lin to find Ah Chang studying her with those rheumy eyes.

"Not yet," she answered. "We've, uh, only been married a short time."

"Ah so." His gaze shifted to Hawk. "Your man, I think, will give you many sons, many daughters."

"That's the plan," she said softly.

Chapter 8

The image of Mei Lin cuddled in Hawk's lap stayed with Gillian throughout the ride to Kowloon's deepwater commercial port. It lingered at the back of her mind during the tour of the gigantic Ching Mai Container Facility.

Hawk had contacted Griff, who'd pulled the necessary strings to hook them up with the Port of Hong Kong's director of security. William T'ang was one of China's new breed of up-and-coming professionals. Still in his late thirties, he sported a Bluetooth phone device hooked over his right ear and two beepers clipped to his belt.

Clearly not happy about the possibility that a person or persons unknown might have breached security at his facility to smuggle animals into a shipping container, he began his briefing with visual references to the wall-size map that dominated his office in the Marine Operations Center.

"Our port has been the world's busiest for many years. We currently operate nine terminals."

He thumped various facilities scattered around Victoria Harbour.

"Our main dockages are here, at Ching Mai. On Stonecutters Island. And this is our newest facility. Altogether, we service more than forty thousand seagoing vessels a year, from supersize oil tankers to two- or three-passenger sampans."

Forty thousand ships! Gillian's gaze shifted from the map to the window. T'ang's office was in Ching Mai's Marine Operations Center, a multistory structure that gave a bird's-eye view of the sea of endless rows of shipping containers she'd spotted from the air.

"How many of those containers can a cargo ship hold?" she asked.

"That depends. As you can see, they come in varying lengths. For international shipping, we measure cargo capacity in twenty-foot equivalent units, or TEUs. Our nine-container terminals alone have a total handling capacity of eighteen million TEUs."

"Yikes! Eighteen million units! How in the world do you keep track of all those?"

"Very carefully." T'ang gave her a thin smile. "And, if I may say so, very efficiently. Our average turnaround time for a container vessel is less than ten hours."

Gillian was impressed. Even more so after he handed hard hats to her and Hawk for their ground-level tour of the operation.

"Hong Kong was one of the first facilities to comply with the International Ship and Port Facility Security Code promulgated in 2004," T'ang informed them. "The process begins at the entry gate."

Wheeling his open-sided vehicle through a canyon of containers bearing familiar labels such as Wal-Mart and Target and Tyson Foods, he pulled up at the main entrance. It reminded Gillian of an automated car wash. Side and overhead beams formed a long tunnel that container-laden trucks passed through at the blazing speed of five or six miles per hour.

"Our Integrated Container Inspection System uses gamma-ray imaging to view the contents of every container passing through the portal," T'ang informed them as he led the way into one of the buildings attached to the tunnel. "We also use radiation screening to check for explosives and optical character recognition to marry the container to its computerized log. Together, these three technologies answer the crucial question of what's inside the box."

What was inside the box presently progressing through the tunnel, Gillian saw when T'ang directed their attention to a monitor showing a three-dimensional cross-section, were flat screen TVs. Carton after carton of 'em, stacked so tightly inside the container there wasn't an inch to spare.

The imagery was incredible. So clear and precise, she expected the screens to flicker to life at any second with mind-blowing displays of color.

"We use portable screening units to check containers loaded or unloaded from ships at sea. The system isn't infallible," T'ang conceded. "Contraband *could* slip through. But the monitors would certainly pick up live animals, moving around in cages, making noise."

"Unless they weren't moving around or making noise," Hawk countered. "They could have been drugged. Or someone could have slipped the cages into a container after it went through screening."

The suggestion that his dockworkers might be engaged in smuggling clearly didn't sit well with the port's security director, but he was realistic enough to admit the possibility.

"We do full background checks on all our operators. That's not to say we can't miss something. Our best defense against the kind of tampering you suggest, however, is the container locking system. It's completely cipher-driven. Once the shipper seals his containers and certifies that they're ready for international transit, only certain officials can decode the ciphers and open the boxes enroute."

"Like who?" Gillian wanted to know.

"Like the people who work directly for me. Our Coast Guard units. Your transportation security agents."

With eighteen million units passing through Hong Kong's port facilities at any one time, Gillian remained skeptical until she got down and dirty in the midst of the terminal.

Diesel fumes belched from the trucks lined up under a massive lift that moved on rails. The lift operator sat in a booth high atop his moving, frame-shaped crane, operating his joystick with astonishing speed and accuracy. While Gillian watched in awe, he dropped a set of giant prongs, clamped them onto a container, swung the box off the truck and deposited it atop a stack of three others.

He emptied the truck within minutes. It drove off and another chugged into place. When the second truck had been unloaded, the lift slid forward on its rails and got ready to unload a third.

The speed and efficiency of the process amazed Gillian almost as much as its computerized mechanization. When she searched up and down the endless rows, the only humans she saw were the truck drivers sitting patiently in their cabs, the lift operators perched high above them, a scattering of cargo managers in hard hats and armed security guards.

After the tour of the main facilities, they jumped a high-speed patrol boat for a trip to one of the massive platforms that loaded and unloaded ships in midchannel. The process was pretty much the same. Cranes removed containers from the ships and loaded them onto marine transporters. The transporters passed through a portable scanning system before transferring the containers to other ships ferrying them back to a land terminal.

By the time Gillian and Hawk parted company with T'ang around 5:00 p.m., she was windblown and salt-sprayed and reeking of diesel fumes. She had also pretty much bought into the theory the infected animals could have been drugged and concealed in a shipping container before it went through screening at the port.

Hawk wasn't quite as convinced. "It might pay to make another visit to the terminal facilities. After dark, and without the director of security looking over our shoulder."

Gillian was mulling over the somewhat daunting prospect of dodging those giant cranes in the dark when they arrived back at their hotel. The same clerk who'd greeted them on their arrival was at the reception desk again. The young woman looked a little startled at the dock smells her guests brought with them but smiled and presented Gillian a note sealed with a red wax chop.

"This came for you. I was just going to send it up to your suite."

"Thank you."

"And thanks for the champagne you sent up yesterday," Hawk added. "We enjoyed it and the fruit tray very much."

Yesterday? Good Lord! Gillian stepped into the elevator with a slight sense of shock. Was it only yesterday they had arrived in Hong Kong? Only last night she'd slapped her champagne glass down on the coffee table and attacked the man beside her? So much had happened in the hours since that she hadn't really let herself think about the fireworks that angry kiss had set off.

She could think of nothing else as the elevator doors pinged shut. Feeling the heat, Gillian unfolded the monogrammed note. Adriana Hall's scent drifted from the thick vellum and penetrated even the eau d'diesel filling the small space. Wrinkling her nose, Gillian relayed the note's contents to Hawk.

"Our friend has just received word that one of Hong Kong's most prominent physicians is putting part of his collection of cloisonné on the market. She's wrangled an invitation for a private showing this evening at seven. With dinner afterward, if we're available. Are we?"

She lifted her gaze, saw Hawk frowning at the flashing floor buttons and waved the note in front of his face.

"Private showing at seven? Dinner afterward?"

Personally, Gillian had had enough of Ms. Hall for one day. She half hoped he would suggest a let's-keep-her-dangling strategy.

"We're available." His mouth took a wry turn. "As long as you refrain from writing out six-figure checks for items you know are fake."

"Be interesting to see if Ms. Hall tries to palm more repros off on us," Gillian agreed as the elevator doors swished open.

Hawk checked his handheld scanner before inserting his key card. Once inside the suite, Gillian tossed the note onto the black lacquer coffee table. The handwriting was as bold and distinctive as the scent.

"Hall has our cell-phone numbers," she mused. "Wonder why she didn't call instead of sending a note?"

Hawk shrugged, clearly more interested in the alignment of the porcelain ginger jars than her idle question. "They're dead center again, damn it."

"Best not to mess with Chinese notions of harmony and balance."

Unconvinced, Hawk prowled through the rest of the rooms. While he checked his other triggers, she unwrapped the package they'd left with the chauffeur. He'd had it delivered to their suite.

The altar was a pretty piece. Not worth a tenth of what she'd paid for it certainly, but the design was well executed and the glaze hand-fired. After careful consideration, she moved the bamboo plant gracing a narrow console table a few feet to the right and countered it with the altar.

Satisfied that she hadn't disturbed the balance of the room, Gillian wandered out on the terrace. The wind off the bay lifted the ends of her hair and played with the flaps of her deep blue cardigan. She had a clean view of the dock area where Adriana Hall's warehouse was located, but the tall buildings of the business district blocked most of the jam-packed Mid-levels. From this distance, she could see only a faint trace of the shacks clinging to the hills above.

Funny how that outdoor escalator had crawled upward with the weight of a thousand years of history on its back, moving from gleaming, twenty-first-century high-rises to dirt-floor shanties that had seen empires come and go. Those one- and two-room dwellings might look like a gray-brown blur from the Peninsula's lofty terrace, but the images Gillian had taken away from her visit were more vivid than any of the others she'd gathered during this jam-packed day.

One in particular stayed with her. She didn't have to close her eyes to summon the picture of Hawk with Mei Lin snuggled in his lap. She was reliving that moment—and Ah Chang's prediction that her man would give her many sons, many daughters—when Hawk joined her on the terrace.

He'd shed his blazer and some of his exasperation with the Chinese passion for neatness and order. The wind ruffled his short dark hair and flattened his tan turtleneck to his frame. Following her example, he leaned his elbows on the rail beside hers.

"Some view, isn't it?"

"Mmm."

She angled her head, debating how much of her thoughts to share with him. The decision came easy when she looked up at the stranger she'd been so certain, so arrogantly and stupidly certain, she knew.

"Speaking of views, I saw a different side of you this morning."

"How's that?"

"You were good with Young Tau."

"He reminds me of myself a few decades back."

"And Mei Lin?"

"She's a little cutie." A smile crept into his eyes. "A lot like another dark-haired beauty-in-the-making I used to know."

Gillian swallowed a sigh. This wasn't the moment to rekindle the anger from last night. Still, she couldn't let the little-girl bit pass unchallenged.

"We didn't know each other when you were Young Tau's age, and I was never as cute or as cuddly as Mei Lin."

"I doubt your father would agree with that."

She refused to debate the issue. She had a more important matter to get off her chest.

"After watching you with those two, I think I owe you an apology."

Confusion and a hint of wariness replaced the smile in Hawk's eyes. "For what?"

"I'm sorry I goaded you last night," she said quietly. "I wanted to force you to see me as I am now, not as the girl I used to be. But it turns out you weren't the only one wearing blinders."

She lifted a hand and stroked his cheek. His skin was warm against her palm, his five o'clock shadow prickly.

"I've seen only what I wanted to see, too. The unflappable Mike Callahan, as cool and in control at the firing range as he is in the field. I haven't really looked for the man under that macho exterior. I don't know him or what he went through when he was Young Tau's age."

"You don't want to know."

"You don't want to tell me," she corrected. "Any more than you want to tell me about the woman you once loved."

Hawk could feel himself stiffening. After all these years, he should have put the past behind him, should have been able to conquer the memories.

"That's okay."

The understanding and acceptance in Gillian's voice made him cringe inside.

"Right now it's enough that you want me," she said. "Almost as much as I want you. I can wait until you realize what we might have together could be as good— or better—than what you lost."

She came up on tiptoe to brush her lips over his. The kiss held none of the fury of last night's, none of the anger or the greedy desire. Yet the whisper-light touch bent Hawk's control to the breaking point.

She had it wrong, he thought savagely. She couldn't feel anywhere near the craving for him that he did for her. It was like a beast in his belly, clawing and snarling for release. He could feel the raw hunger tearing at his insides.

He'd unleashed the beast once, and listened to its

agonizing death rattle amid the roar of chopper blades and stutter of gunfire. He couldn't, he *wouldn't,* let his hunger for Jilly dull his instincts or put her in danger.

The need to protect her, to spare her the kind of agonizing death Diane suffered, went beyond thought or reason. She didn't want to hear that, though, any more than he wanted to tell her about Diane's agonizing death.

He owed her a response, however. Owed her the truth after her quiet offer to wait.

"Listen to me, Gillian." Clamping his hand over hers, he flattened it against his cheek. "You're nothing like her. You're everything that's bright and beautiful in this world. She was… She was…"

Clever. Mercurial. A fire in his blood.

"She was like me," he said finally. "Different background, different path to law enforcement, same gut-deep craving for something we never quite found together."

"What kind of something?"

"I don't know. Contentment, I guess is the best label for it. Joy in little things like reading the Sunday paper or sharing a meal we didn't have to cook over a can of Sterno."

"Or having sex that wasn't spiked by danger?"

"That, too," he admitted.

"Hmm." She thought for a few moments. "We may have a problem."

As if that was news to Hawk. Hadn't he been trying to tell her for weeks now that he wouldn't fit into her world or she into his?

"I might not give you that 'something,' either," she

said with a small frown. "The only part of the Sunday paper I read is the book-review section. I rarely cook, and when I do, it's not over a can of Sterno. As for sex…"

The frown dissolved into a smile that looped Hawk in knots from the neck down.

"I have a feeling we'll both find what we're looking for there, with or without the danger."

He almost lost it then. The woman tempting him with that smile was all Gillian. Salty and wind-tossed and more aromatic than usual but unmistakably Gillian.

A trill of ascending notes was the only thing that kept Hawk from burying both hands in her hair and covering her mouth with his. It took a second shrill ring to get him to back off completely.

With a muttered curse, Gillian went inside to retrieve her cell phone. Hawk followed in time to see her make a face when she identified the caller.

"Yes, Adriana, we received your note. It was waiting when we got back to the hotel a few minutes ago."

She listened a moment, one dark brow lifting.

"No, we didn't go antique hunting after we left you this morning. I decided to show my husband some of the city."

The term came more easily to her, Hawk noted. The knowledge pleased him in a way he wouldn't let himself think about right now.

"We're thrilled about the private showing tonight," Gillian was saying. "Thanks for arranging it. Black tie? We can do that. Good. Fine. See you then."

She flipped the phone shut. There was no explanation needed for the call, as he'd overhead the conversation, and no going back to those moments before it.

The grim business that had brought them to Hong Kong had returned to center stage.

"Adriana says she'll pick us up in forty minutes. We'd better get cleaned up."

Chapter 9

While Hawk showered in the guest bathroom, Gillian took over the dressing room in the master suite. She intended to use every one of the allotted forty minutes to arm herself for her second session of the day with Adriana Hall. She was damned if she'd go the neat and demure route this time. Not with Hall doing her exotic Suzie Wong imitation.

Field Dress hadn't included a slinky *cheongsam* in Gillian's wardrobe for this op, but they had raided one of D.C.'s trendiest boutiques. The strapless bustier was made of blonde lace and cut straight across her breasts. The matching bikini panties showed more creamy flesh than they covered. The lacy garter belt clipped on to stockings that added a lustrous sheen to her legs.

Over the decadent undergarments, she wore a slim, ankle-length skirt slit high on one side and a tuxedo-style jacket, both in tawny gold velvet. The fabric was whisper-thin and as soft as milk against her skin. The gold Guiseppe Zanotti heels that completed the ensemble roused instant lust in her heart.

Even before she strapped on one of the three-inch sandals, Gillian knew she'd have to reimburse the government for these babies. For the whole outfit, she decided as she made a slow pirouette in front of the mirror. No way was *any* of this going into Field Dress's storage vault.

She kept the jewelry simple—gold earrings, the jade charm, the wedding ring—but went all out with her makeup. Mahogany shadow, a darker shade of liner and two coats of mascara deepened her eyes to blue smoke. Pale blush with just the faintest glitter of gold dusted her cheeks. Her lip gloss was a cool sherry. To emphasize the long, straight column of skirt and jacket, she swept her hair up and anchored it in a cluster of curls atop her head. Only a few tendrils escaped to feather her nape and brush against her cheek.

Hawk's low whistle when she joined him in the sitting room more than justified the extra time in front of the mirror. He'd put some effort into his appearance, too. His tux was shadowy black, a dramatic contrast with her shimmering gold.

Darkness and light. Heaven and earth. Fire and water.

The East was weaving its spell on her, Gillian thought as Hawk did an approving walk-around. She didn't need the spark that leaped along her nerves to know deep inside they could come together eventually, yin to yang, male to female. Now all she had to do was convince Hawk of that.

"Did Field Dress come up with that outfit?"

The husky edge to his voice upped her yin level by a factor of ten. "They did."

"Remind me to give them my personal thanks when we get home."

"I intend to do better than that. I'm going to write out a check for everything you see here and one or two things you don't."

Okay, maybe she shouldn't have tacked on that provocative remark. She and Hawk had stirred so many emotions out on the terrace it probably wasn't wise to add to the mix.

She could wait, she reminded herself sternly. Sooner or later he'd bury his past. When he did, they would forge a future. Together. She could wait.

Or not.

Her carefully scripted scenario went all to hell when Hawk slid his palm around her nape and played with one of the long, loose tendrils.

"Do you remember when you tapped me to escort you to that Washington soiree? The one where I wanted to hook up with Congressman Kent?"

Like Gillian could forget? That was her first semi-official date with Hawk. True, she'd more or less coerced him into using her as entrée into the tight-knit community of Washington's elite. Also true, he'd abandoned her when he spotted his prey. Until he had, however, she'd feasted on the sheer excitement of walking into a crowded room on his arm and the smooth play of muscle and tendon under the sleeve of his tux.

"You wore your hair up that night, too."

The rough pads of his fingertips raised goose bumps on the back of her neck.

"Did I?"

"All I wanted that night was access to Kent. Yet all I could think about was the curve of your neck. The way these loose curls teased your jaw."

And how much he'd ached to spring the silky mass free of the confining hair clip and watch it tumble over her naked shoulders.

Hawk had known then Gillian-with-a-J was trouble as far as he was concerned. Only now did he realize just how serious that trouble was.

"We'll talk," he promised. "As soon as this op is over."

When he had her home.

Safe.

And in his bed.

There was something different about Mike Callahan and his pseudo bride. Adriana sensed it as soon as they joined her in the limo.

It wasn't just their physical appearance, although Gillian Ridgeway's seductive elegance produced an instant spurt of envy. Adriana tried to tell herself any woman could achieve that combination of sultriness and sophistication given enough time and money. Look at what she herself had accomplished with a few stolen millions.

With a hidden smile, she slid her fingertips along the deep, slashing V of her gown. She'd opted for Western dress tonight: a designer label she could never have afforded on her paltry government salary. The halter top bared most of her cleavage. A dog collar of sparkling crystals concealed the wound left by the bullet that pierced her larynx.

Would Mike notice? She'd make sure he did. She'd certainly noticed his attire.

Adriana had never seen him in formal dress. He'd been in Special Ops when they'd worked their first op together in Afghanistan. She'd been part of a DEA task force that was supposed to convince the United States' supposed allies to cut back on their poppy production. Sergeant Mike Callahan had been in charge of task force security. Even decked out in Kevlar and coated with dust, the man was hot.

They'd hooked up several times after that, each meeting more explosive than the last. The woman Adriana once was had convinced herself she'd found her match. Then Callahan left her to die in that sweltering green hell.

This was the same man, she reminded herself fiercely as he stretched out his long legs beside Gillian's. He might have traded his jungle BDUs for a starched white shirt and hand-tailored tux, but it was the same man.

"I'm glad you were available on such short notice," she purred.

"So are we," the Ridgeway woman replied, shifting to snap on her seat belt. The movement bared her left leg below the knee and several inches above. "Tell us about this doctor who's putting part of his collection up for sale."

"Alexander McQuade is quite a character. A hard-liner who opposed returning Hong Kong to China right up until the Union Jack came down in 1997. I didn't know him then, of course, but I've procured several items for him in recent years."

She kept her voice pleasant and her gaze on Gillian's face, but she didn't miss the hand Mike laid on his "wife's" knee. The gesture was so casual—and so possessive—that Adriana felt herself stiffening. But it wasn't until Gillian answered the gesture with a slanting sideways glance that she began to suspect there was more between these two than she'd realized. Something sour churned in her belly as she tipped Ridgeway a cool smile.

"Are you as knowledgeable about cloisonné as you are about ceramic altars, Gillian?"

The zing hit home, although the brunette tried not to show it. Ridgeway knew she'd been fleeced on the altar, and the fact that she did added another level to this cat-and-mouse game they were playing.

"More so, as it happens."

The response was as barbed as the question.

"During my stint as a Cultural Exchange officer, I convinced the Beijing Museum of Arts and Crafts to put together a traveling exhibit of antique cloisonné pieces. It toured the U.S. for eight months. Most people prefer the blue of the Jingtai era, but I have to admit I'm particularly addicted to the red and green patterns developed at the court of Emperor Jong Te."

Well, well. So the woman had claws and wasn't afraid to show them.

"Are you familiar with their spread-wing dragon patterns, Adriana?"

The pointed query necessitated a quick retreat. She'd taught herself enough about Oriental antiques to demand ridiculous prices for the pieces she hunted down for collectors, but she was no expert on any particular school.

"Not as familiar as I should be," she answered with perfect truth. "It sounds as though you and Dr. McQuade will hit it off rather well. Mike and I will have to entertain each other while you two talk colors and dynasties."

Which suited her plans perfectly. She wanted Callahan to herself so she could twist the knife a little before thrusting it home.

As Adriana had anticipated, Alexander McQuade found an instant soul mate in Gillian. He barely gave her time to take a sip of the perfectly chilled white wine his butler served before stubbing out his black cigar and thumping his own tumbler of scotch onto a side table.

"You've a liking for the Jong Te era, do you? Wait until you see my phoenix vase. It's the centerpiece of my collection."

He practically dragged her to the upstairs gallery that ran the length of his home in one of Hong Kong's older and exorbitantly expensive neighborhoods. Adriana took advantage of the opportunity to slide her arm through Callahan's. Her steps were slower going up the wide oak stairs, her smile deliberately seductive.

"Your wife is quite charming."

"I think so," Callahan answered, his gaze on the pair ahead. A seemingly accidental press of her breast against his arm jerked his attention back to Adriana.

"How did you meet?"

"Her father asked me to teach her to shoot."

Adriana would keep that in mind. If Mike Callahan had instructed Ridgeway, the woman would know which end of a weapon was which.

"Perhaps you could give me some pointers. It's been a while since I got out my gun." Particularly since she'd become so adept with a knife.

"What kind of weapon do you shoot?"

"A SIG Sauer P226."

The flicker of surprise in his hazel eyes gave Adriana a vicious satisfaction.

Did I trigger some memories, Callahan? Are you remembering that the P226 is standard issue for U.S. Drug Enforcement Agency officers?

"That's more gun than most women want to handle," he said slowly.

"Perhaps, but then I make it a point not to conform to expected standards."

She got to him. She didn't have any doubts on that score. Yet when Gillian negotiated the purchase of a cloisonné vase and a pair of candlesticks from McQuade and their host led the way back downstairs, Callahan seemed to slip away from her.

The other dinner guests arrived before Adriana could reel him back to her side. She didn't ignore the people seated on either side of her at the table groaning with silver candelabra, but her focus never left Mike or his partner on this op. By the time Adriana stuck her fork into a puffy Yorkshire pudding, she'd finally interpreted the pair's private signals.

Gillian Ridgeway was in love with Callahan. She disguised it beautifully with her new-bride patter and the frequent touches expected of a recently married woman, but Adriana had learned to interpret the most subtle signals.

She'd had to, first during her DEA days, then to survive those brutal months with a drug lord who needed to inflict pain to receive pleasure. She'd turned the tables finally and derived more pleasure than she'd ever imagined from watching the pig die. Slowly. Agonizingly. To this day, she wasn't sure whether he'd bled out from the knife she slid between his ribs or suffocated on the testicles she'd cut off and stuffed in his mouth.

Or maybe it was the shock of learning that she'd watched him through eyes swollen almost shut from his blows. That all the while she'd crouched in a corner, she'd listened to his drunken boasts about the millions he and his cohorts had reaped in profit over the years. That she'd used the codes he'd stupidly taped to the shelf above his computer to access his account and transfer those millions to a secret account she herself had set up.

Slitting Charlie Duncan's throat had given Adriana almost the same thrill. Duncan hadn't recognized her. Not until that last moment, when his blood gushed over her hand. In his last frantic seconds, he'd tried to tell her that he thought she was dead, that he'd checked her pulse.

The gutless, lying bastard! She hadn't lost consciousness. Not for a moment. She'd almost drowned in her own blood from that shot to the throat, but she hadn't blacked out. She knew Charlie Duncan hadn't come within ten feet of her, let alone checked her pulse.

Nor had Mike.

Her eyes narrowed on him across the table, so rugged, so masculine with those wide shoulders and that cool, don't-mess-with-me smile. She wouldn't have believed he'd leave her. Even now it was like a steel-toed boot to her midsection.

While the candles flickered and crystal sang, Adriana savored her imminent revenge like the other guests savored McQuade's forty-year-old Bordeaux.

She'd make her move tomorrow, she decided. She'd continue the farce, take Callahan and his "bride" on another buying expedition and torment Gillian Ridgeway by seducing the man she hungered for. The man who had once hungered for *her*.

Then she'd end the game.

Several hours later Gillian tossed her evening bag on the coffee table of their hotel suite. The beaded crystals hit with a sharp snap.

Hawk gave her a quizzical glance as he deposited the carefully wrapped cloisonné pieces beside the bag. "You haven't said a word since Adriana dropped us off. Is something bothering you?"

"No."

She dragged in a breath. Let it out with a huff.

"Okay, yes. That woman was all over you like a bad rash."

"What?"

"Adriana. She had her hands on you all night."

"No, she didn't."

"Let's just do a recap, shall we? There was that little

arm squeeze when we went upstairs at McQuade's. The palm she ran up between your shoulder blades after dinner. The hip nudge when we got into the limo for the ride back to the hotel."

"There was a hip nudge?"

"Don't play coy with me, Callahan." She folded her arms. Above them, her blue eyes flashed a warning. "If you expect to pull off this pose as a brand-new husband on a honeymoon buying spree, you'll have to at least *pretend* some interest in your bride."

"Pretend? Jesus, Gillian. We must have inhabited alternate universes tonight."

As irritated at the grilling as he was aroused by the rise and fall of her breasts above those crossed arms, Hawk yanked his white tie out of its bow.

"Couldn't you tell I spent my entire evening trying to keep *my* hands off *you?*"

"Actually, I couldn't."

The tone was still pure acid, but some of the belligerence went out of her stance. Only some. Adriana Hall had obviously sparked a temper Hawk had witnessed only in brief flashes before.

"Tell me this," she demanded, one foot tapping. "Did you or did you not pick up on the tension that crackled through the air whenever she got within ten feet of you?"

"If I felt any tension, it was because she's still our only link to Charlie Duncan and the black marketeering case he was working when he was murdered."

Gillian tapped her foot again. Every feminine instinct she possessed told her the blond bombshell wanted more than a business arrangement from Hawk. The woman oozed sex from every pore. Did Hawk honestly not see she had her claws out? Was he that zeroed in on their mission?

Had he really spent the whole evening trying to keep his hands off *her?*

The admission went a long way toward putting a cap on Gillian's simmering irritation. Still, she and Ms. Hall were going to have a serious discussion in the not so distant future. Right now she needed to make her position clear to her husband, pretend or otherwise.

With a swish of velvet and nylon, she crossed the room and caught the dangling ends of his tie. "You said earlier that we'd talk when this op was over. I'll hold you to that. In the meantime…"

She yanked on the tie and tugged him down to her level.

"Keep this in mind the next time Adriana rubs up against you."

She should have expected the sizzle. After all, she'd initiated the contact. Yet the voltage lit her up, inside and out. This was their third kiss, but who was keeping count? All Gillian knew was that she'd never get enough of his taste, his touch.

She pulled back, breathing hard. Her hunger was reflected in Hawk's narrowed eyes and the rigid set to his neck and shoulders. He'd kept his hands to himself, although his fists were balled and the knuckles showed white.

Torn between satisfaction at the sight and guilt at tempting him, she left him there in the living room.

She could wait, Gillian reminded herself. Grinding her back teeth, she changed into the negligee and cleaned off her makeup. She could wait, she repeated as she crawled into bed. She could wait until Hawk buried his past.

He'd damned well better get on with it, though.

Chapter 10

Hawk stood with his tie hanging loose and his fists bunched. He heard water splash in the bathroom. Drawers slam in the bedroom. Gillian's mutter just before she flicked off the bedroom lights.

Stillness settled over the suite. Still he didn't move. He knew damned well that if he so much as twitched a muscle, he'd storm into the bedroom and feed the savage hunger Gillian's kiss had roused.

The minutes ticked by. Five. Ten. When he was sure he had himself under control, he hit the suite's well-stocked minibar. He poured one shot and made sure it lasted until he was certain Gillian was asleep.

He cracked the bedroom door to check. She was curled on her side at the edge of the wide bed. Her black hair spilled over the pillow she'd punched up under her cheek. Her slow, regular breathing confirmed she was out for the count.

Easing the door shut, Hawk went into the dressing room and ripped off the tie. His tux jacket hit the floor. The white dress shirt followed. Moments later he was in a dark T-shirt, jeans and a black leather bomber jacket. His Glock nested in its holster, a familiar weight at the small of his back. He had to get out, had to release some of this tension before he blew. Jaw tight, he stalked back into the sitting room and activated his transmitter.

"OMEGA control, this is Hawkeye."

"Yo, Hawk. Ace here."

Griff sounded wide-awake. He must have just come back on the control desk. With all the time zone changes, it was still yesterday in D.C.

"What's happening, buddy?"

"I've decided to pay a late night visit to the container facility we toured this morning."

"You see something there that looked suspicious?"

"No, which is why I'm going back. Any operation that large and complex has to have some holes."

"Roger that. Jade providing backup?"

"Negative. She'll remain here at base. I'll brief you if I find anything."

He signed off, hoping to hell his instincts proved true. He craved action, the more physical the better. Nothing would give him greater pleasure right now than to come face-to-face with human slugs engaged in black marketeering.

* * *

Hawk slipped out the hotel's back entrance and hailed a cab. He had the driver drop him off at a dingy-looking dive he'd noted about a mile from the container terminal. The flyspecked neon sign advertised beer in both Chinese and English. The fog of cigarette smoke that rolled out when he opened the door was as noxious as the reek of stale sweat.

Inside, a motley collection of truckers, dockworkers and sailors off ships flying flags from around the world crowded small tables or stood with elbows planted on the bar. Hawk's entry turned few heads in this polyglot gathering. He wedged in at the bar and ordered a Tsingtao.

It took two of the potent brews to settle on his mark. The dockworker was big, beefy and just this side of falling-down drunk. He was Chinese but complained loudly in broken English to two sailors nursing their beers about his prick of a boss.

"Not good enough we stack containers in straight line, many, many high. No, no. The son of a turtle says wrong place. Must move all."

"Yeah, you've told us."

"Many hours to move, no extra pay. Son of a turtle."

The mariners grimaced. "Give it a rest, mate, and 'ave another beer."

"Son of a turtle."

Lurching to his feet, the dockworker stumbled to the men's room. Hawk followed. A long piss and a wad of Hong Kong dollars later, he'd convinced the man to show him how and where someone without a security pass and enough interest might access the terminal.

The dockworker sobered a little when the night closed around them. He started to get downright nervous when they approached the terminal. In keeping with its 24/7 operation, high intensity spots flooded the entire yard and lit up the front gate, where trucks were lined up to pass through screening. Cold mist seeped in off the ocean as Hawk and his now-reluctant guide skirted the gate and followed the wire-topped, fifteen-foot-high chain-link fence.

"There," the man grunted, pointing to where the fence made a ninety-degree right turn. "Hole in lights."

He was right, Hawk saw. Although video surveillance cameras and bright floodlights swept the area, the floods only overlapped at the outer rim of their arc. Closer in, at the corner of the fence, was a patch of inky blackness.

"I go now."

The dockworker took off, disappearing into the night, and Hawk settled in to wait.

He didn't wait long.

The shadows came out of the mist. Dim and shapeless at first, they gradually resolved into a string of five or six hunched figures, some carrying what looked like bundles.

As Hawk watched, the lead figure signaled the others to wait while he crept up to the fence. He crouched there for long moments, watching, listening, waiting for the accomplice that finally ducked out from behind a row of containers.

After a whispered exchange, the accomplice stood guard while the first man slipped what looked like a crowbar from under his padded jacket and used it to pry up the lower portion of the fence. Holding the fence up with one hand, he beckoned urgently to the others waiting in the shadows.

Hawk lifted his wrist to within an inch of his mouth. "OMEGA control, this is Hawkeye."

"We read you, Hawk."

"Get on the horn to Will T'ang, director of security for the Port of Hong Kong."

The crouching figures crept forward, one by one, a line of dim shadows in the mist.

"Tell T'ang he's got a perimeter penetration approximately two hundred yards west of the main gate, where the fence makes a turn to the north."

"I'm on it."

The first man had crawled through, but the chain links appeared to have snagged the second. The individual with the crowbar struggled to lift the fence higher.

"I'll stay in position until… Hell!"

The metal rod snapped out of the holder's hands and came down with a sickening thud on the trapped penetrator.

"Aieeeee!"

His agonized cry ricocheted through the night. He twisted frantically, but the chain link prongs only gouged deeper into his flesh.

"Ay! Ay!"

His screams unleashed a frenzy of activity as the others rushed to his aid. All except one. The individual who'd wielded the crowbar took off like a shot.

Hawk was up and after him in the next breath.

* * *

Dawn was just beginning to streak the night sky when Hawk deactivated the alarm and used his key card to access his hotel suite. He still reeked of stale cigarette smoke. Damp earth was smeared across his face and skinned knuckles. The bastard who'd wielded the crowbar hadn't gone down easy. Thank God!

Hawk could have prevented the brutal exchange of blows. He knew enough dirty moves to disable any opponent without breaking a sweat. His only excuse for wading in was that he'd craved the action…and the physical release that came with it.

The subsequent hours with Will T'ang and the port police had added to his satisfaction. The scum Hawk had taken down admitted to being part of a people-smuggling operation and implicated a number of others—including the VP of a shipping agency who'd provided him and his pals with the necessary codes to unlock the containers.

The downside to the night was that none of the persons interrogated admitted to involvement in the black-market animal trade. Still, Hawk thought as he moved through the darkened suite, he now had a hard link to at least one smuggling ring. If the police shook these characters hard enough—and Hawk intended to see that they did—one of them might make the connection to another….

A soft snick froze him in his tracks. He was in the gun business. He recognized the sound of a round being chambered when he heard it.

"Turn around. Very slowly."

"Jesus, Jilly!" Relief crashing through him, Hawk swung toward the sound of her voice. "It's me."

A lamp clicked on. Light chased away the predawn darkness and illuminated the woman in the high-backed wing chair. Above the distracting V of her negligee, her face was as cold and hard as the blue steel Beretta she had aimed at his chest.

"You want to point that away and engage the safety?"

"I don't think so."

"Jilly—Gillian," he corrected hastily. "Ground your weapon."

For an incredulous moment, Hawk thought she'd ignore the safety drill he'd pounded into her.

He sucked in a swift breath, and let it out again when she downed the Beretta, thumbed the safety, ejected the magazine and emptied the chamber. Even without the loaded weapon, the atmosphere in the suite was lethal.

"Where were you?"

"I paid another visit to the container terminal."

"And you didn't think it was necessary to advise me of your intentions?"

"You were asleep."

The feeble excuse only compounded his sins. Hawk recognized that even as her eyes narrowed to slits.

"From the blood on your face and hands, I have to assume you connected with someone or something."

"I connected," he confirmed. "If you'll call room service and order some hot coffee, I'll clean up and tell you what went down."

"Order your own damned coffee."

"Lighten up, Gillian. I told you when we left Ching Mai that the terminal warranted another visit."

"Yes, you did," she acknowledged icily. "But you failed to mention that you didn't consider me necessary for the return trip."

Hawk wasn't used to being grilled by a rookie…especially one with a tangle of dark hair tumbling over her bare shoulders and her skin gleaming through the lace of her gown.

"Look, I may have screwed up by going solo on this one but…"

"There's no 'may' about it, Bubba."

"…but," he continued, working hard to contain his annoyance, "I opened a lead. I'll tell you about it after I clean up."

He picked up the phone and ordered the coffee on his way to the shower.

While Hawk occupied the walk-in glass stall with its panoramic view of a city just coming awake, Gillian changed into a military-style tunic and slacks in regimental red. The jacket's high collar and elegant fit had come from the hand of an exclusive designer. The martial style highlighted by shoulder epaulets and gold piping more than matched Gillian's mood.

She'd conquered her anger by the time Hawk re-emerged, but hurt and disappointment still bit at her like angry wasps. He met both head-on with an apology.

"You were right. I *did* screw up. I'm sorry."

She nodded stiffly. "Apology accepted. On one condition. I want the truth, Callahan. Why didn't you wake me and tell me what you planned? Were you playing the big, strong protector again? Making sure little Jilly didn't get her hands dirty? Or were you just worried that I'd get in your way?"

"None of the above. I had to get out of here for a few hours, Gillian. If I didn't, I would have ended up putting my fist through the wall."

"What? Why?"

She saw the answer in the hot glance that raked from her neck to her knees.

"Oh."

"Right. Oh."

Well, crud! Now she felt not only hurt but stupid. And guilty. She'd *had* to yank on his tie last night. *Had* to give him something to remember the next time Adriana Hall rubbed up against him.

"I guess I owe you an apology, too."

Hawk's grim expression lightened, and something close to a smile edged his mouth. "Not hardly, babe. There's the coffee," he added when the doorbell buzzed.

How did he do it? Gillian wondered ruefully as he headed for the door. One minute, he had her steaming. The next, she was putty in his bruised and battered hands.

Which, she thought while he tipped the waiter, might be a tad difficult to explain to Adriana Hall when they met with her for another buying expedition later.

Gillian didn't comment on that fact until he'd downed some caffeine and briefed her on his nocturnal activities.

"So," she summarized as the sun made a valiant attempt to burst through the drawn drapes, "you might have a line on a smuggling operation, but our only direct link is still Adriana Hall's export operation. Which means, unfortunately, we'll have to spend more time with the woman. How are you going to explain those?" she asked with a nod at his skinned knuckles.

The issue didn't seem to worry him. Shrugging, he inspected his hands. "We went out for a nightcap after Adriana dropped us off last night, chose the wrong section of Hong Kong and I had to muscle our way out."

There it was again. Tough, macho husband taking care of the little woman. Gillian felt her back teeth grinding.

One of these days, she vowed, she'd smash that mold for good.

"Don't forget," she reminded him, "Ah Chang and the kids are meeting us here this afternoon."

"Right."

"I wonder if Young Tau has sniffed anything out."

"He might have," Hawk said wryly, "if he's got the same nose for trouble I did at that age."

Although Gillian had *not* been looking forward to another buying expedition with Adriana Hall, the session produced unexpected results.

After purchasing an ancestor painting depicting the history of a family named Hu, several scrolls of calligraphy art and an antique snuff bottle, Gillian fell completely and utterly in love with a pair of temple dogs reported to be from the residence of a powerful, seventeenth-century courtier. They were cast in bronze, about five feet high and, in Hawk's opinion, not exactly friendly looking. Gillian, stroking a hand over the cool bronze, tried to infuse him with some of her enthusiasm for the pair.

"You place them outside, at the front door, to ward off evil spirits."

"They'd probably do a pretty good job of scaring off delivery men and mail carriers," Hawk drawled, eyeing the snarling teeth.

"See how the male's raised left foot rests on a rounded sphere? It represents the worldly possessions of those who live in the house."

He duly noted the sphere. An amused Adriana stayed in the background with the shop owner.

"This one's the female. Her right foot rests on the belly of a baby temple dog, representing the home and…and family."

Hawk caught the slight hesitation and had a pretty good idea what was behind it. Despite the rings circling their fingers, he and Gillian didn't have a home or a family for these bizarre creatures to guard.

Something shifted inside him. He never let himself think about the cesspool he'd come from. He was younger than Young Tau when he'd lit out on his own—and twice as belligerent. Thank God for the judge he'd been hauled in front of in that grim Montana courthouse. His Honor had turned him over to the recruiter who promised the military would kick the smart-ass street punk out of him. And kick it had. Hawk grew up in a hurry. In the process, he'd found a band of brothers. Special Ops took care of their own.

So did OMEGA. Nick Jensen had recruited him during the long convalescence after the botched op in

Central America. Hawk had needed the change, needed a new focus to numb the still-searing memories.

That was *all* he'd needed until Gillian Ridgeway had forced her way into his world. Now he couldn't think beyond getting her in bed, sliding his palms over her breasts and belly, burying himself in her heat.

The idea of making a home with her, of starting a real family, hadn't even entered the equation. Until now.

Cursing under his breath, he swung toward Adriana. "How much for the pair?"

She was in business black today. Tailored suit with a skirt cut above the knees. Spike heels. Pale blond hair swept up in a smooth twist and anchored with an ebony clip. Lifting a brow at Hawk's terse query, she consulted with the shop owner.

"His asking price is fifteen thousand dollars."

"U.S. or Hong Kong?"

"U.S."

Gillian nudged him with an elbow and issued a gentle warning. "Careful, darling. If these are the real thing, which I think they are, we'll need a certificate of authenticity and documentation that the sale conforms to Chinese laws on the export of antiquities."

Adriana gave her a cool smile. "Naturally, I would make sure those are provided." Her glance slid back to Hawk. "If you're serious, you should counter. I'd suggest twelve thousand."

"Tell him eight. Cash."

"He won't take that!"

"Tell him."

* * *

They settled on ten-five, with the heavy bronze dogs to be delivered to Adriana's warehouse for packing, crating and shipping.

"I'll need to cash a check," Hawk informed a delighted Gillian. "Why don't you take the car and our other purchases back to the hotel? I'll meet you there."

"You sure you don't need me to go to the bank with you?"

"I can handle it. And we're expecting visitors, remember?"

Adriana's pulse jumped. They'd just handed her the opening she'd been waiting for.

"I'll go with him," she told his pseudo wife. "By the time we return, the necessary documentation should be ready. I'll make sure your husband gets back to the hotel."

The offer wiped some of the delight from Gillian Ridgeway's face.

She knows, Adriana thought gleefully. She knows Callahan and I share some kind of connection she can't quite put her finger on. It isn't physical. Yet. But she's worried it could be.

And so it will.

Something dark and sexual stirred in Adriana's belly. The bastard who'd kept her chained to his bed had taught her to satisfy him in ways Gillian Ridgeway could never imagine. Ways *she'd* never imagined.

The memory of those brutal lessons fed her craving for revenge. She'd have Mike Callahan on his knees. She'd make him groan and beg for release. He wouldn't get it, but he *would* pleasure her over and over again before she sent him back to the hotel with the yeasty scent of sex clinging to his body.

She would take immense pleasure from throwing the fact that Callahan had betrayed her in Gillian Ridgeway's face. Then, at last, Adriana would exact her revenge for the betrayal that had robbed her of her soul.

Chapter 11

Gillian returned to the hotel with the day's purchases, minus the bronze temple dogs. The doorman extracted the packages from the backseat of the limo and informed her she had visitors.

"They arrived about fifteen minutes ago."

"Thank you. Would you have these packages taken up to our suite, please?"

"Certainly."

She made a concerted effort to smooth her frayed nerves as she crossed the lobby and hurried toward Ah Chang and the children. Adriana Hall could put Mother Teresa's teeth on edge, and Gillian certainly didn't qualify for sainthood. Something had to break on this op, and soon, or she would strangle the predatory blonde.

Mei Lin saw her coming and popped out of her chair. "Jill-An! *Nee hao?*"

"I'm very well, thank you."

Scooping up the girl, Gillian gave her a warm hug. Mei Lin was in her pink sneakers and grungy jeans, topped by a slightly frayed brocade jacket that Gillian guessed was probably her Sunday best. The girl returned the hug but was clearly disappointed not to see Hawk.

"Where is Cal-Han *Shen-Sheung?*"

"He'll be here shortly," Gillian promised as she hooked an arm around Young Tau's shoulders.

The boy looked startled and a little embarrassed at the contact. He, too, had spiffed up for the visit. His hair was slicked down and he wore a cable-knit sweater several sizes too large for his thin frame. Gillian hitched Mei Lin on one hip and greeted Ah Chang.

"Honorable Grandfather, I apologize most sincerely for not being here when you arrived."

He accepted the apology with a gracious nod.

"Would you like to take tea here in the lobby, or shall we have it upstairs where it's a bit more quiet?"

High tea at the Peninsula was a world-renowned institution. A string quartet played in the upper gallery, while waiters in impeccable white uniforms wheeled carts loaded with an incredible selection of tea cakes, finger sandwiches and scones with clotted cream. Because it was *the* place to see and be seen, however, it was crowded and usually required a long wait to be seated. Gillian was prepared to offer the headwaiter an exorbitant bribe for a table when Ah Chang opted for a more private setting.

"We should go upstairs, yes? So I may examine the items you intend to buy?"

"Very well. I've made a number of purchases," she told him as she escorted the group to the elevators, "pending your approval."

Gillian set Mei Lin down and offered Ah Chang her arm to the elevators. Once on her floor, she almost forgot to deactivate the intrusion-detection system Hawk had set when they left and had to fumble in her purse. The device brought a leap of avid interest to Young Tau's eyes.

"You have iPod? You listen to Chao Tsai?"

Gillian was very familiar with the first Chinese rock band to burst on the scene in the late nineties. She'd attended one of their concerts in Beijing. Despite the government's suspicion of Western-style heavy-metal rock, Chao Tsai—Overload in English—was still going strong.

"I love Chao Tsai," she told the boy. "I don't have any of their music on this device, but I have several of their CDs at home."

The naked envy on Young Tau's face spurred an instant decision to procure him an iPod loaded with songs from his favorite bands before she left Hong Kong. She'd splurge on Mei Lin, too, Gillian decided as she inserted the key card. New jeans, fuzzy pink sweaters, a warm winter coat. And hair ribbons. Or barrettes. And dolls. Maybe a stuffed bear and...

"Ai-yah!"

Young Tau followed his exclamation with a long, low whistle. His sneakers squeaking on the foyer's marble tile, he led the way inside. He stood small and thin and almost lost in the luxuriousness of the suite as he made a slow circle to take it all in.

Mei Lin wasn't particularly impressed. She skipped inside and scrambled onto the couch, making herself at home. Gillian escorted Ah Chang to a comfortable chair before shedding her jacket. The hotel's efficient staff had already delivered her packages. They waited on a side table along with her purchases from last night.

"Let's order tea first, shall we? The hotel has a fine selection. Do you have a preference, Honorable Grandfather?"

She started to hand Ah Chang the room service menu but realized the cataracts clouding his eyes must limit his sight. Maybe she could arrange to have those taken care of, too, before she left.

"May I read you the brands?"

At his nod, she ran through the extensive list. Ah Chang stroked his wispy beard and pondered his choice for several moments. Selecting tea was serious business in China. Choosing from the Peninsula's incredible medley made it a matter of grave consideration.

He settled at last on Snow Bud, a delicate white tea made from the leaves grown in the highlands of Zhejiang Province. Gillian placed the order and added an assortment of cakes, pastries and sandwiches to accompany it.

When Gillian retrieved her purse to get some money for a tip, the holstered subcompact tucked into a side pocket gave her pause. She didn't *think* either of the kids would go through her bag, but she couldn't take the chance.

The holstered gun went into the suite's safe before she showed a curious Young Tau and Mei Lin around. The wide terrace with its plants and bubbling fountain delighted the little girl. Young Tau glommed onto the brass telescope set on its wooden tripod in front of the windows.

"Look! I see the elevator to Mid-levels. It climbs the hill like silver dragon. Look, Mei Lin."

He boosted up the girl and balanced her on his knee so she could peer through the eyepiece.

Watching them, Gillian felt her heart turn over inside her chest. The boy couldn't be more than nine or ten, yet he'd become the protector of a child who, according to Ah Chang, was no relation. How would either of them survive if the man who'd taken them in succumbed to age or disability?

Ah Chang followed her gaze. As if reading her mind, he exhaled a small sigh. "I, too, worry for them."

His rheumy eyes followed the children as they explored the console that controlled the flat-screen plasma TV.

"Young Tau does much to put food on our table," Ah Chang murmured. "I fear he may pick the wrong pocket one day, however, and I will not be able to help him."

"Perhaps my, uh, husband can talk to him."

Damn! She was sure she'd progressed beyond stumbling over that word.

"Mike had it rough as a child, too. He doesn't speak of those years, but I suspect he can share his hard-earned wisdom with Young Tau."

Along with the fund the Callahans would establish. Gillian had already decided it would pay a monthly living stipend for both children's upkeep. She was still mulling over how best to go about setting it up as she unwrapped her purchases for Ah Chang's inspection.

The ancestor paintings and calligraphy art she'd picked up this morning won an approving nod, as did the antique snuff bottle with a winter scene painted on the inside with incredibly delicate brushstrokes. Ah Chang brushed a loving hand over the cloisonné vase she'd purchased from Alexander McQuade last night, but the three-foot-high candlesticks drew an exclamation of delight.

With a little grunt, he lifted one of the heavy pieces and squinted at the intertwined dragon and phoenix depicted in exquisite enamel. "Very old," he confirmed. "Very fine. How much you pay?"

He didn't so much as blink at the five figures Gillian quoted.

"Good price. You bargain well. But you must have papers to take these pieces out of China."

"They're being prepared."

Room service arrived at that point. The tall candlesticks held places of honor on the coffee table as the waiter wheeled in a cart. The assortment of cakes and tea sandwiches made Mei Lin squeal with delight and Young Tau gape in openmouthed astonishment. Both children waited to dive in, however, until Gillian had tipped the waiter and poured a cup of Snow Bud for Honorable Grandfather. The pale amber blend gave off a floral aroma with just a hint of nutty undertone.

Ah Chang's seamed face folded into lines of sheer ecstasy at his first sip. He savored the moment with eyes closed. When he opened them again, the children were quivering like greyhounds at the starting gate. At his nod, Young Tau attacked the cart. Mei Lin was more dainty in her approach but still managed to pile her plate high.

Gillian held the plate for her while she scrambled onto the sofa once again. Her stubby legs stuck straight out. Pink sneakers bobbing with impatience, she waited while Gillian spread a napkin across her lap, then reached for her plate of goodies. Her first choice was a cucumber-and-shrimp sandwich cut in the shape of a heart. Flicking off the dill sprig adorning the shrimp, she gobbled up the heart and looked to Gillian with a question in her black eyes.

"Where is Cal-Han *Shen-Sheung?*"

Good question, Gillian thought as she filled a plate for Ah Chang. Where the hell was Callahan?

"McQuade messengered over the documentation for the cloisonné pieces early this morning. I can't believe I forgot to bring them with me."

Trailing the scent that stabbed at Hawk's memory like a serrated knife, Adriana led the way across the tiled foyer of a pricey, waterfront high-rise.

"How fortunate my condo is only a few blocks from the bank. It won't take a moment to retrieve the papers."

Hawk merely nodded as she jabbed the button for the thirty-fifth floor. After an hour with Adriana, his internal alarms were pinging like hell. What he couldn't decide was whether the warning signals were due to her less-than-subtle sexual overtures or his growing conviction she was tugging on invisible strings in a determined attempt to keep him and Gillian dancing to a tune only she could hear.

Although he'd downplayed Gillian's biting criticism of Hall last night, Hawk wasn't dead from the neck down. His senses had registered every careless brush of Adriana's arm or leg, every throaty laugh.

In another time, another place, he would have jumped on her unspoken invitation. She was the kind of woman who'd once pushed every one of his buttons. Smart. Supremely self-assured. Cool on the outside, molten at the center. Yet Hawk felt only relief when the elevator disgorged them on the thirty-fifth floor.

"This is me."

She keyed the lock of a door painted dragon-red and framed by a black lacquer oval. The interior of the palatial condo reflected the owner's complex personality. The furnishings were Asian but sparse and dramatic. The floor tile, sofa and chairs were stark white. The tables and chests and desk that stretched along one wall were black lacquer. Slashes of red and thick area rugs in rich colors put Adriana's sensual stamp on the place.

Tossing her purse on a table, she headed for the intricately carved chest that dominated one wall. The doors folded back to reveal a high-tech entertainment center on one side and a bar racked with gleaming crystal decanters and glasses on the other.

"How about a drink?"

"It's a little early for me."

"It's always five o'clock somewhere."

Hawk went still. Absolutely still. As if from a

distance, he heard Diane Carr echo the title of the Alan Jackson–Jimmy Buffet classic.

She'd thrown the line out so often it had become a joke between them. Yet the DEA agent knew how to hold her booze. She never worried about the time and would toss back a shooter when and where she wanted. That last mission, before she and Hawk and Charlie Duncan went into the jungle, she'd damned near drunk them both under the table.

An ache started in Hawk's chest, squeezing his lungs, constricting his air. He could still see Diane in that smoky dive, her hair a short, shining cap of red, her gray eyes mocking as she and Charlie went at it again. They'd never clicked, she and Duncan. Hawk usually ended up having to referee arguments that too often went from friendly to downright hostile.

"I'm having a scotch on the rocks."

He dragged himself from that small, dank bar and locked on the woman who sent him an over-the-shoulder glance.

"Sure you don't want something?"

"Maybe I will. Scotch is good."

Hell! His hands were shaking. What was wrong with him?

Adriana Hall was nothing like Diane Carr. The face, the frame, the voice, the accent, the mannerisms—all different. Even their style of dress. When Diane wasn't in jungle or desert gear, she lived in jeans and tank tops. Adriana was always in silk, with high mandarin collars and side slits designed to make a man sweat. Yet…

What were the odds that the widow of a British Lord who'd spent most of her life in Asia could quote Alan Jackson and Jimmy Buffet?

His thoughts chasing after themselves, Hawk suddenly remembered the gap. After Lord Hall died, his widow dropped out of sight for almost eight months. She'd resurfaced in Hong Kong, a silent partner in Wang and Company. Griff was still digging into that gap. He would have contacted Hawk if he'd come up with anything.

Those eight months were front and center in Hawk's mind when Adriana handed him a heavy crystal tumbler.

"What shall we drink to?" she asked.

"How about old friends…and new acquaintances."

"Is that how you regard me? As a new acquaintance?"

"We don't fit the old friends category," he said slowly, tipping his glass to hers.

The scotch burned a line down the back of his throat. Hawk welcomed the kick as Adriana's green eyes challenged him over the rim of her glass.

"There *is* the possibility," she murmured, "we might become more than friends."

"I don't think so."

"So quick, so sure." Her lips curved in a mocking smile. "Too quick, perhaps?"

"Are you forgetting Gillian?"

"Ah, yes. Your bride."

She took a long swallow of scotch, making perfect semicircles of red on the tumbler, then set it on a round-topped drum table.

"Rest assured, I haven't forgotten Gillian. I simply

consider her, shall we say, extraneous. What happens
here, between us, has nothing to do with her."

"Nothing's going to happen between us, Adriana."

"So quick, so sure," she repeated with that taunting
smile. "Is it me you're afraid of? Or yourself?"

He couldn't get the Jimmy Buffet song out of his
head. He had to know, had to kill the absurd thoughts
that kept pushing at the edges of his reason. Hawk could
think of only one way to deep six them.

Deliberately, he let his gaze roam from Adriana's red,
glossy lips to her throat to her full breasts. When his eyes
met hers again, he saw himself reflected in the dark pupils.

"Hell, yes, I'm afraid. Of you...and of how much I
could want you."

She didn't try to disguise her triumph. It glowed in
her face and threaded through her husky laugh. "Let's
see how much that might be."

She flattened her palms on his chest, slid them
upward, curved them over his shoulders. Her perfume
gnawed at his senses.

Hawk banded her waist and drew her against him.

He had to know.

Her hands locked behind his neck. Their bodies fused
at hip and thigh. With her three-inch heels, Adriana
didn't have to stretch to reach his mouth. Her lips moved
over his, seeking, demanding.

Slowly, Hawk reached up. He gripped her wrists,
unlocked her hold and brought her arms down. "I can't
do this, Adriana."

Her eyes narrowed. "Actually, you were doing it
quite well."

"I won't do it," he amended.

"Why not?" She wrenched free of his hold. "You can't tell me you don't want me. And you certainly can't pretend you're in love with your 'wife.'"

She spit the word out, her tone every bit as acid as Gillian's when she'd warned Hawk that Adriana was putting the make on him.

"Oh, Christ," she muttered when he refused to respond to her taunt. "You *are* in love with her."

Disdain flashed in her eyes, followed by something heavy and dark. Hawk used that as his exit cue.

"I'd better go."

He swung toward the door, and the abrupt turn brought him into contact with the drum table they'd set their drinks on. He made a grab at the table before it toppled but missed. Pale gold scotch spewed, and the tumblers hit the tiles with the splinter of breaking glass.

"I'm sorry." Hawk went down on one knee to gather the sharp pieces. "Get a towel, and I'll wipe up this mess."

"Don't bother."

"You could cut yourself."

Stacking the larger pieces, Hawk carried them to the wastebasket beside her desk. A detour to a kitchen outfitted with gleaming white tile counters and black appliances produced a hand towel in hand-stitched linen.

The smaller pieces joined the larger in the wastebasket. The sopping linen went into the sink. Only then did Hawk nod to the woman who was still standing where he'd left her.

"You nailed it, Adriana. I am in love with Gillian. If

you want the truth, I didn't know what love was until she came into my life."

Her nostrils flared, but she didn't say a word as he let himself out.

The moment the elevator doors closed, Hawk signaled OMEGA control.

"Yo," Griff answered. "What can I do for you?"

"I want pictures of Lord Hall's wife. Some shots taken immediately before his death."

"We can manage that. I'll have the computer guys do a search of the Singapore social scene."

"E-mail them to me as soon as you get them."

"Will do. Anything else?"

"Yeah. Get on the horn to DEA. See if they still have the DNA profile for Special Agent Diane Carr on file."

"Special Agent Diane Carr. Got it."

Hawk reached in his pocket and carefully withdrew a glass shard. The glossy lip print looked as red as blood.

"I'm overnighting a DNA sample to you. Run it against Carr's. I need the results, like, yesterday."

"Roger that."

The glass shard was in his pocket when he exited the elevator and had the doorman hail a cab.

He still wasn't sure. Everything in him said Diane *couldn't* be alive. He'd watched her die, choking on her own blood. She *couldn't* have risen from her dank, green grave and taken on the form and face of Adriana Hall.

He might have convinced himself, if not for that kiss.

His eyes bleak, Hawk tipped the doorman who held the cab's door open for him.

"Where shall I tell the driver you wish to go?"

"The airport."

The hotel could probably arrange a courier and overnight express service. Or one of OMEGA's contacts in Hong Kong. But a grim sense of urgency drove Hawk. He had to see this glass shard get on a plane himself.

Then he needed to sit down with Gillian. He couldn't let his past destroy her.

High above, Adriana stood at the window and watched the cab cut into the bumper-to-bumper traffic.

He loved her.

He didn't know what love was until she came into his life.

The bastard! The lying bastard!

How many times had he backed *her* against a wall and yanked down her jeans or BDU pants? How many times had she locked her legs around his hips and ridden him with unrestrained greed? How many nights had they flopped down in a tangle of limbs, breathless and limp and sweaty?

And he didn't know what love was until that blackhaired bitch came into his life?

Seething with a fury so raw it all but consumed her, Adriana stalked into her study. Her hand shook as she slid back a small wall panel to reveal a safe. Inside was a selection of disposable cell phones and the electronic device that disguised her voice.

She stabbed in the number she knew by heart. When a voice answered in the guttural Cantonese of the streets, she replied in kind.

"Where is the woman?"

"At the hotel."

"You're sure?"

"We've been watching both exits."

"Take her! I want it done today." Adriana's knuckles were white where she gripped the phone. "Watch yourselves. She may be armed. Just be sure you deliver her alive."

She snapped the phone shut, still shaking with fury.

The game was over.

Chapter 12

Gillian caught her cell phone on its second ring.

"Mrs. Callahan."

She didn't stumble. Playing Hawk's wife not only came more easily now, it was starting to feel almost natural.

Almost being the key word, of course. There was still the slight matter of consummating the vows they hadn't exchanged.

"It's me," Hawk growled into her ear.

"Finally! Where are you?"

"Stuck in traffic. I have been for the past half hour."

"I hope you're on your way back to the hotel. We finished tea some time ago, Honorable Grandfather has inspected our purchases, and Mei Lin keeps asking for *Callahan Shen-Sheung*."

"I'll be there as soon as I can. I have to make a quick trip to the airport first."

"Huh?"

"I may have something. I'll tell you about it as soon as I get back. Right now, my priority is to get a DNA sample on a plane and on its way to the OMEGA labs."

Gillian felt her jaw sag. Where in the world had he acquired a DNA sample?

"The traffic's hell. It may take an hour or more to make the round trip to the airport. Can you keep Honorable Grandfather and the kids occupied until I get there?"

Gillian glanced at the trio. Ah Chang's hands were tucked in the sleeves of his blue jacket. His chin had sunk almost onto his chest. He was ready—more than ready—for an afternoon nap. The kids, on the other hand, had polished off the cake and most definitely needed to work off their sugar high.

"I'm sure I can convince Ah Chang to stretch out on the bed while I take the kids for a walk. We might hit a few stores while we're out."

"Sounds like a plan. Just stick to the main thoroughfares. I'll be back as soon as I can."

Gillian hung up, feeling just a tad guilty. She'd left Hawk with Adriana. He'd intended to make a quick trip to the bank and be back at the hotel in fifteen or twenty minutes. When those minutes had stretched into an hour, then into two, she'd started to wonder.

Okay, she'd done more than wonder. She'd begun to think some very nasty thoughts about a certain predatory blonde who couldn't seem to keep her hands to herself.

From the sound of it, Hawk had either dumped Adriana or used her to uncover this DNA sample he mentioned. Wondering what the heck that was all about, Gillian slipped her cell phone in the pocket of her slacks and approached Ah Chang.

"Honorable Grandfather, my husband just called. He's been delayed but hopes you and the children could wait and have dinner with us. Would you care to lie down on the bed and rest while I take the children out to visit a few shops?"

Young Tau and Mei Lin gave the plan a hearty endorsement. In the face of their eager enthusiasm, Ah Chang made only a token protest before allowing Gillian to show him to the second bedroom. She made sure he had everything he needed for his comfort, then grabbed her purse.

"All right, kids. Let's do it!"

She couldn't wait to hit Nathan Road! She'd have to curb her buying urge, though, and get them what they needed, not what she'd like them to have. Jackets, she decided. New jeans. Long-sleeved shirts and sweaters in preparation for Hong Kong's cold, damp winter. Warm socks. New underwear. A stuffed elephant or monkey for Mei Lin. An iPod for Young Tau, loaded with songs by Chao Tsai and every other Chinese rock band in existence.

So stuffed elephants and iPods didn't fall into the "need" category? What good was the fat savings account she'd built up during her years with State if she couldn't blow it on friends and family?

She and Young Tau negotiated the lobby with Mei

Lin between them. The girl clung to their hands, and every other step was a skip or a hop. When they approached the front door, one of the Peninsula's smartly uniformed bellmen tugged on the tall brass door handle.

"Would you like a car, madam?"

"No, thanks. We'll walk. We're just going one block, to Nathan Road."

Young Tau's face fell a little as he took in the fleet of Rolls-Royces parked at the ready.

"I'll send you home in one," Gillian promised. "The driver will take you and Mei Lin and Honorable Grandfather right to the Mid-levels."

The three strolled down the hotel's curving walk. When they hit the crowded street fronting the harbor, the stiff breeze blew Gillian's hair into her eyes. She tossed her head to clear her vision and caught a jerky movement from the corner of one eye. Swinging around, she saw only a mass of humanity behind her. All of Hong Kong, it seemed, was out this afternoon.

With a smile of anticipation, she led the kids across an intersection, around the corner and onto the street of one of the world's great shopping meccas.

Gillian couldn't remember the last time she'd had so much fun. She had four shopping bags draped over one arm. Mei Lin and a stuffed panda occupied the other.

Young Tau strutted beside them, showing off his American Eagle hoodie and the white wires sprouting from his ears. An accommodating clerk at the Apple store had used the gift card Gillian purchased to download a hundred of the boy's favorite songs from iTunes. The shopping bags that Young Tau carried swung to the beat of Chao Tsai's latest hit.

Her arms ached, but Gillian needed to make one more stop. She'd spotted an optometrist's sign in one of the shop-lined alcoves leading off Nathan Road. Luckily, it was only a few doors down from a Ben & Jerry's.

More sugar—what the hell.

She found an empty booth and deposited Mei Lin, her panda and the collection of shopping bags. Young Tau emerged from his music long enough to make his selection from the gargantuan menu listing flavors in English and Chinese. Mei Lin took longer. *Much* longer. After considerable debate, she settled on a scoop of Cherry Garcia.

"Wait here for me, okay? I'm going in that shop." Gillian pointed to the store at the rear of the alcove. "I'll be right back."

As expected in a Nathan Road optometrist's shop, the window displayed frames by Calvin Klein, Christie Brinkley, Donna Karan and Oakley, to name just a few of the top designers. Gillian wasn't interested in frames. What she wanted was the name of a reputable ophthalmologist who could remove the cataracts clouding Ah Chang's vision.

The optometrist was more than helpful. She left the shop a few moments later with a list of three top surgeons. She'd check out each one personally, she decided as the shop door snicked shut behind her, and…

"Excuse me, madam." The man came out of the shadows at the back of the alcove. "You want hand-tailored dress? Very elegant suit?"

"No, thanks."

"I am excellent tailor." He planted himself in front of her, smiling. "Just come. Look at my work."

"No, thank you. I have all the dresses and suits I need."

She tried to go around him, but he was persistent.

"Just come, look my shop. I sew for children, too." He nodded toward the ice-cream shop where Mei Lin was waving her spoon at Gillian. "Make very special *cheongsam* of finest silk for little girl."

Gillian hesitated, wavering. "All right, I'll look."

She held up a finger to let Mei Lin know she'd only be a moment and followed him through an arched opening. All she saw was a row of trash containers lined up along an alley.

"Where is this shop?"

"Just here, madam. Just here."

"Sorry, I don't have time to go farther."

She spun on her heel, made one step and took a crushing blow to her temple. Her knees crumpled. The world went black.

"Ai-ah!"

Mei Lin's high-pitched cry pierced Young Tau's musical haze. Jerking upright, he yanked out an ear bud.

"Why do you screech like a rooster with its tail feathers plucked?"

"Jill-An!" Mei Lin aimed her spoon like a sword. "Jill-An fall. Two men pick her up. Carry her away."

Young Tau leaped out of his seat and crashed through the front door. Her panda forgotten, Mei Lin darted after him. He skidded to a stop in the center of the alcove and spun in a circle.

"Where?" he shouted at Mei Lin.

She wielded her spoon again, her hand trembling. "There!"

"Go back to the hotel!" Young Tau raced for the alley. "Tell Honorable Grandfather!"

He didn't stop to ask if she could find her way. She'd wandered the back alleys and prowled the tourist haunts with him since the day he'd found her, huddled beside a battered suitcase in an out-of-the-way corner of the Ferry Terminal. Hungry and frightened, she didn't know how long she'd been there. Many, many hours, she thought.

Who had left her there, and what had happened to them, Young Tau never discovered. He'd taken her to Honorable Grandfather. Ah Chang had made inquiries but found no answers. When he suggested turning Mei Lin over to the authorities, the girl had cried and clung to Young Tau like a small, frightened crab.

No, he had no worry that Mei Lin would find her way back to the hotel. What scared him to the soles of his sneakers was what might have happened to Jill-An. Hong Kong presented a gleaming face to the world, but Young Tau knew all too well there were still dark, reeking dens that wise men would be well to avoid at all costs. He also knew young, beautiful women like Jill-An had been known to disappear, sucked into the sex-slave trade that flourished despite every attempt by international authorities to stamp it out.

Under his new hooded sweatshirt his heart was hammering, as he raced for the far end of the alley. The sound of an engine gunning added a kick to his step. He burst onto a narrow side street just as a truck pulled away from the curb. It was a small lorry with a roll-up rear door, the kind that made deliveries to shops all over Hong Kong.

Panting, Young Tau swung in a circle. When he saw no sign of Gillian, he started after the truck.

Thank the gods for the drunken dragon that was Hong Kong's traffic! It lumbered forward, lurched to a halt, rolled ahead again. Young Tau darted across three lanes, dodging taxis and lorries and commuters, keeping the truck in sight. His heart jumped into his throat when it edged into the lane leading to the high-speed tunnel connecting Kowloon and Hong Kong Island. Once it hit the tunnel, it would pick up speed and Young Tau would lose it.

First it had to clear the massive construction project at the west end of the Harbor Promenade!

Legs pumping, Young Tau cut left and ran for the spot he knew constituted the worst bottleneck. Four lanes of traffic merged to two as vehicles crawled under a new overpass that was still just a framework of steel girders and half-poured cement. Prominently placed signs warned that this was a construction zone with restricted entry. Ignoring the signs and the shouts from workers in hard hats, Young Tau darted onto the half-finished overpass.

He crouched behind a girder as the truck approached so the driver wouldn't see him. At the last minute he dropped like a lychee nut and spread-eagled himself across the roof of the back compartment. His acrobatics didn't go unnoticed. Horns honked and the driver of the car behind the delivery truck stuck his head out the window. But by then the truck had cleared the construction. Speeding up, it entered the lane heading for the tunnel.

Mei Lin's sneakers slapped the circular walkway leading to the hotel. Her heart was bursting inside her chest. Her breath came in ragged gasps.

She recognized ornate doors and the man in the tall hat who opened them. She knew that beyond those doors was a vast lobby filled with marble columns and potted plants where she, Young Tau and Honorable Grandfather had waited for Jill-An. She also knew they had taken an elevator to Jill-An's pretty rooms. But what elevator? What rooms?

She'd ask the man in the tall hat. He would know. He *had* to know.

She plowed through a group of businessmen strolling down the walkway and darted right into the path of a taxi pulling up the circular drive. Mei Lin froze. The taxi screeched to a halt. A door sprang open.

"Mei Lin!"

With a sob of joy and desperation, she recognized the deep voice. "Cal-Han *Shen-Sheung!* Someone take Jill-An!"

Hawk didn't understand anything except the names, but the little girl's distress plunged a knife into his gut. Swinging her into his arms, he spun toward the doorman.

"What's she saying?"

Shaking, sobbing, Mei Lin poured out a torrent of Chinese.

"She says… She says someone has taken your wife."

"Where! When!"

The doorman fired the questions at Mei Lin. Clinging to Hawk, she alternated between speech and sobs.

"A few moments ago," the doorman translated, "on Nathan Road. She says she runs right away to tell Honorable Grandfather. She says someone called Young Tau goes to look for Jill-An."

"Ask her if Honorable Grandfather is in our suite?"

"She says he is," the doorman responded a moment later.

"Take her upstairs." Hawk thrust the girl into his arms. "Tell her to wait with Honorable Grandfather. And have someone from the hotel stay with them."

There was a chance Young Tau might call the suite. If so, Hawk wanted someone there who could relay the call. Grabbing a pen from the doorman's pocket, he scribbled his cell-phone number on the closest printable surface, which happened to be the back of the man's hand.

"Here's my number. Tell them to call me immediately if they hear from Young Tau."

He sprinted for the cab that was still idling, the passenger door hanging open, and shouted to the bewildered driver.

"Let's go."

"Where?"

"Nathan Road until I tell you otherwise." Slamming into the backseat, he keyed his Rolex. "OMEGA control, this is Hawkeye. Come in."

"We read you, Hawk."

"Have you heard from Jade?"

"Negative."

"Can you get a GPS fix on her?"

"Not unless she transmits a signal."

An iron band clamped around Hawk's chest. This was what had kept him awake. This was what had gnawed at his insides. Gillian could be hurt. She could be lying in some dark alley, bleeding, choking, gurgling his name with her last...

"Why do you need a GPS fix?" Griff asked sharply. "What's going down?"

The questions yanked Hawk from the inferno of his fears. His chest so tight he had to fight for breath, he keyed the Rolex.

"Jade may have been abducted."

Gillian jolted awake on a shaft of pure agony. Gasping, she lifted a hand to her temple. For reasons she couldn't quite comprehend, both hands came up.

It took her several confused moments to realize her wrists were taped together. Several more to associate her body's seemingly uncontrolled jouncing with the fact that she was stretched out in the back of a vehicle moving over a bumpy road. A paneled van, she discerned when the agonizing pain subsided enough for her brain to resume functioning, or delivery truck of some sort.

If it was a delivery truck, she thought as the fog cleared a little more, she was the only delivery. Her heart thumping as painfully as her head, she struggled to sit up. That was when she discovered her ankles were taped, as well.

A sudden thought speared through the confusion and incipient panic. Mei Lin! Young Tau! She'd left them sitting at the ice-cream shop. They must think she'd deserted them.

Fury gave her a sudden surge of strength. If anything happened to those kids, the bastard who'd whopped her over the head would pay, and pay dearly.

Her anger conquered the pain. She rolled onto her side, searching for her purse. Her cell phone was in her bag…but not her neat little subcompact. Crap!

Only after she'd made a futile search for her purse did she remember the jade pendant. She'd tucked it inside the red tunic.

It was still there, she discovered on a rush of relief. She could feel it against her breast.

With a fervent prayer of thanks that her abductor had taped her hands in front instead of behind her back, Gillian yanked at the tunic's gold buttons. Her clumsy efforts popped the first one off. The second slipped out of its hole. Digging inside the gap, she fumbled for the pendant and felt for the right squiggle.

"OMEGA," she whispered. She didn't think the driver could hear her through the front panel, but she wasn't taking any chances. "This is Jade. Come in, please."

She waited for a response, straining to hear over the roar and thumps of road noise. With a muttered curse, she remembered she had to press twice to receive.

Griff's terse voice jumped out at her. "…from Hawk that you may be in trouble. Please advise as to your situation."

"I'm in the back of what looks like a delivery truck. My wrists and ankles are taped, and I have the mother of all headaches, but I'm otherwise okay."

"We have a fix on your signal. We're tracking you via GPS as we speak. I'll advise Hawk of your direction and notify the Hong Kong police. Can you describe the van? Make? Color?"

"All I can see is the inside of a gray box. The walls have side metal struts with loops. For cargo restraints, I guess. There's one of those roll-up metal doors at the rear."

"What about the driver? Can you see him or anyone else in the front cab?"

"No, the box doesn't have a window."

"Okay. Hang loose while I contact Hawk."

Like she could do anything else?

Then again, maybe she could. The prospect of flopping around in the back of a truck, waiting for Hawk to ride to her rescue, didn't particularly appeal to her.

Scrunching and stretching, Gillian crabbed her way to the side of the compartment and used a strut to pull herself upright. The edge wasn't very sharp, but it was the only edge available. Raising her wrists, she sawed them against the strut.

The tape was tough. That black electrical stuff. Her jaw set, Gillian dragged her wrists up and down. The friction heated the metal. The tape, as well. With a leap of excitement, she saw a tiny cut appear.

She bunched her muscles and tugged. The cut stretched into a deeper V but didn't give. She started sawing again and was concentrating so hard Griff's terse report made her jump.

"Hawk's on your tail. He's ten minutes behind, fifteen at most. I've also given the Hong Kong police your speed and direction."

"Roger that."

"You're picking up lingo. Good goin', Jade."

She knew Griff's approval stemmed less from her grasp of spy talk and more from relief she hadn't succumbed to screaming, hyperventilating hysteria. Gillian didn't rule that out as a possibility, however.

"Can you get to your weapon?" Griff wanted to know.

"Uh, negative."

She didn't really see the point in admitting she'd tucked the Beretta in the safe and waltzed out of the hotel unarmed. Biting down on her lower lip, she attacked the strut again.

"What's that noise?" Griff asked sharply.

"Me. Grunting. I'm sawing…this tape…against the… Yes!"

With a flex of her arms, she parted the bindings.

"I've got my wrists free! I'm working on my ankles."

"Better work fast," Griff advised grimly. "I'm looking at a satellite map and I think I see where you're headed. There's a dockyard dead ahead. If I'm right, the truck will slow for the gate."

She felt the deceleration even as he spoke. With a yank that took some of her skin with it, Gillian got the damned tape off her ankles. She scrambled up, grasping the struts again to steady herself as the truck made a left turn and slowed to a crawl. A few moments later, it stopped.

"I've got you, Jade." Griff was calm and steady, with none of his usual drawl. "Hawk and the cops are just minutes away. Just stay calm."

"Calm. Right."

Gillian's heart pounded. Sweat pooled on her palms.

It was too late to play possum. The shredded tape would give her away in a second.

Flattening herself against the side, she edged closer to the roll-up door. A sick feeling swirled in her stomach when the metal rattled upward.

The two thugs who peered into the compartment didn't see her right away, but Gillian spotted the club one of them wielded. It was thick and heavy and had no doubt left a permanent dent in her skull.

The sight of the billy club steadied her skittery nerves. One way or another, the sleazoid was going down!

They spotted her then. Their eyes widened when they saw she'd freed herself, but it didn't faze them for long. The larger of the two thugs hooked a hand impatiently.

"Come out, woman, or we will come in to get you."

She didn't move.

"Come out!"

The distant wail of sirens broke the standoff. The men looked at each other, startled and obviously unsure what that wail signified but galvanized into action.

"Get her!" the bigger of the two snarled. "Drag her out!"

His cohort reached for a handhold and had a leg up when something dropped from the sky. Thudding into him, it slammed him to the pavement.

"Son of a turtle!" Screaming insults, a furious Young Tau pummeled the man's head and face. "Son of a she-dog!"

Gillian and the second abductor recovered from their

astonishment at the same moment. He swore and swung his club. She leaped forward and swung her foot.

Her ankle boot clipped him right under the jaw. His head snapped back with a neck-cracking crunch. Grunting, he sank like a stone.

Chapter 13

Hawk's taxi tore into the dockyard mere seconds before a flotilla of police cars.

He leaped out of the cab, his weapon drawn and murder in his heart, and took in the scene at a glance.

One man was on the ground. Another lumbered to his feet. Young Tau was on the beefy thug's back, his skinny arms windmilling. As Hawk closed the few yards to the truck in a dead run, the man shook Young Tau off like a pesky puppy.

"Freeze!"

Hawk's shout rifled through the air at the exact moment Gillian popped into view, swinging a billy club like a baseball bat. The thug went down like a stunned ox.

His heart hammering, Hawk reached Gillian's side.

"You okay?"

Her chest heaved under her red jacket and an ugly bruise was forming on her temple, but below the bruise her eyes were alive with glee.

"I'm fine. Did you hear that whop? I gotta tell you, Hawk, it felt *good!*"

He stared at her incredulously, his adrenaline at full boil. Far from the terrified woman he'd expected, Gillian-with-a-J had swung the weighted club by its rawhide loop like a friggin' majorette twirling her baton. Hawk opened his mouth, snapped it shut and turned to Young Tau. Snagging the boy's arm, he helped him to his feet.

"How about you, kid? Are you hurt?"

"Pah!" The boy landed a swift kick in the ribs of the man Gillian had flattened with the club. "This pig no can hurt Young Tau."

Hawk should have felt nothing but relief. He should have thanked the kid for whatever crazy stunt he'd pulled to stick with Gillian. All he could do was clamp a hand on Young Tau's shoulder and squeeze it.

Later that evening, Hawk's thoughts were as gray and as stormy as the thunderclouds that had piled up above Victoria Peak.

After a long session with the Hong Kong police, he'd brought Gillian and Young Tau back to the hotel. They related their adventures to Ah Chang and Mei Lin while Hawk sent a doorman to retrieve the purchases abandoned at the ice-cream shop. After treating the trio to a sumptuous feast at the Peninsula's magnificent rooftop restaurant, they'd sent them home in a limo with promises to see them again before they left Hong Kong.

It would take more than dinner and a couple of drinks to unkink Hawk, however. His mind still churned with unanswered questions, not the least of which was who'd orchestrated Gillian's abduction.

Neither of the men who'd snatched her knew who hired them. The order came from a nameless, faceless caller who used a device to disguise his voice. The number on the thug's cell phone traced to a disposable phone that didn't return a signal. Hawk would bet it was already at the bottom of Victoria Harbour.

Nor did the men know the reason behind the abduction. After some intense interrogation, though, the big, surly one admitted he'd snatched other women for the sex trade. Some he'd picked at random off the street. Others had been selected to fit precise criteria. Gillian, he'd assumed, fell into that category, since the person who'd hired them had described a blue-eyed, black-haired Caucasian and directed them to watch her specifically.

They'd been paid half the agreed-on sum in advance. Bundles of bills had been left at various locations. The Hong Kong police had promised to check out every location in the hope someone had noticed whoever made the drop. Hawk didn't hold out much hope they'd get a break. Whoever was behind the aborted abduction had covered his tracks too well.

Then there was this business with Adriana. Gillian's kidnapping had shoved it right out of Hawk's head. Only now, with Hong Kong's spectacular light show bathing the skyscrapers across the harbor in a rainbow of brilliant colors, did he again think the unthinkable.

Which was why he was somewhat less than responsive when Gillian sashayed out of the bedroom, ready to rehash the afternoon's events. She was all warm and cuddly after a shower and wrapped in one of the hotel's plush robes. She was also still pumped by the fact that she and Young Tau had taken down two heavies.

"I just about lost it when Young Tau dropped out of the sky like that. I can't believe he jumped onto the top of the truck and rode it through the high-speed tunnel."

"Me, either," Hawk growled.

His stomach twisting at the thought of what could have happened to both Young Tau and Gillian, he shoved his hands in the pockets of the jeans he'd changed into while she was in the shower. With everything that had happened today, his mood was too edgy and his temper too close to the surface for worsted wool and cashmere.

"I have to tell you," Gillian said as she tested the purple bruise on her temple with a fingertip, "swinging that billy club gave me one intense jolt of satisfaction."

"Yeah, well, watching you swing it scared the hell out of me."

She blinked at the curt response. Hawk knew he should throttle back. She'd held her own today and then some. The mere fact that she'd *had* to still had him rattled.

"What if you'd missed?" he told her. "The goon you attacked must have weighed two-fifty or more. If your swing had gone wide, he could have slammed you against the truck and broken every bone in your body."

"Then it's a good thing my swing *didn't* go wide," she said stiffly.

"Griff told you I was right on your tail. All you had to do was stall for a few minutes."

"Oh, sure! A nine-year-old takes on two kidnappers and I'm supposed to stand there, wringing my hands and waiting for you to ride to the rescue, while they beat him to a pulp." Exasperated, she yanked on the belt to her robe. "Why don't we talk about what's really bugging you?"

"You think you know what's bugging me?"

"I've got a good idea. You still don't believe I can take care of myself—or my partner—in the field. Obviously this afternoon didn't settle any doubts."

"I might feel a little better about this afternoon if you hadn't waltzed out of here unarmed."

The sarcastic retort raised spots of red in her cheeks. She'd only admitted she'd left the Beretta at the hotel after he'd insisted she report it missing along with her purse.

"As it turned out, I didn't need the Beretta."

His answer to that was a disgusted snort.

"So what's it going to take for you to trust me, Hawk? Do I have to kill someone? Put a bullet between his eyes or strangle him with my bare hands? Rip out his heart? Eat it raw?"

"Now you're being childish."

"No, now I'm pissed."

Her eyes were as stormy as the clouds that had begun to dump sheets of rain. The drops splattered against the windows as Gillian crossed her arms.

"Let's just review the bidding here, fella. True, I let myself get snatched in broad daylight. Also true, I was

weaponless at the time. But I was far from helpless. I
sawed through the tape, clipped one of my kidnappers
under the chin with a well-placed foot and coldcocked
the other. I think I did pretty damned good. So would
you, if you'd stop brooding long enough to admit it
turned out to be a pretty exciting afternoon."

"Exciting? You thought getting kidnapped was
exciting?"

"Terrifying and mortifying *and* exciting."

The last remnants of Hawk's self-restraint snapped.
He'd done everything in his power to dissuade Gillian
from getting into this business. Even here in Hong Kong
he'd tried to his damndest to shield her. Yet she refused
to stay in the safe, secure niche he kept shoving her into.

"You want excitement?" His fists closed around her
upper arms. "I'll give you all you can handle."

Her head went back. Her astonished gaze locked with
his. Hawk knew she could read his intentions in his face.
He waited, giving her an out. Two seconds. Three. Then
he yanked her against him and crushed her mouth with his.

Everything inside Gillian leaped with joy. At last! She
wasn't sure how she'd finally broken through his defenses,
but this wasn't the time to stop and analyze the situation.

Flinging her arms around his neck, she matched his
violence with her own. Her mouth ground against his. Her
hips thrust forward. They were belly to belly, her breasts
pancaked against his chest, her breath coming in short, delighted gasps, when Hawk swung her into his arms.

He kicked the half-closed bedroom door and sent it
back on its hinges. She was already tearing at his shirt
as he strode across the room. The buttons parted and

gave her access to his chest. Gillian swept her hand over the planes and contours, her stomach rolling in wild anticipation.

He dropped her on the bed and ripped off his shirt. His jeans hit the floor. She waited, one leg bent, her entire body screaming, until he came down beside her on the silken coverlet and unbelted her robe. The flaps parted, and Hawk's breath left on a hiss.

"You're lucky I didn't know you were naked under that thing," he said, his voice hoarse. "You would've never made it to the bed."

"I don't have any objection to floors or sofas."

Or any other surface, horizontal or vertical, that would give them the necessary leverage.

"I'll remember that," Hawk muttered.

He skimmed a hand from her throat to her breasts to her belly.

"Christ, you're beautiful. Like a porcelain figurine. Smooth and delicate and perfect."

Uh-oh. Gillian didn't like where this was headed. The *last* thing she wanted right now was for Hawk to decide she was some kind of fragile Dresden doll that required careful handling.

"Perfect, huh? I'll remind you of that when you poke me awake and tell me to roll over so I'll stop snoring."

"You snore?" he said absently, more interested in the dark triangle between her thighs.

"My sister says it's more of a snuffle."

His hand trailed over her mound. Gillian let her legs part.

"I, uh, also hate sharing my French fries," she warned

on a breathless note. "You get your own, Callahan, or you don't get any."

His fingers burrowed into the silky hair. A half smile tugged at his lips.

"I'll get my own. Anything else?"

He slipped a finger inside her, then another. His thumb pressed the sensitive bud. The exquisite sensations shot straight from her belly to her brain.

"Nothing you need to worry about right now!" she gasped.

Arching, Gillian gave herself up to his touch. He used his hands, his mouth, his teeth, driving her to a near frenzy. Amid the spiraling pleasure, one thought kept repeating.

Hawk. This was Hawk. She'd hungered for him for so long, ached to feel his body crushing hers. The sheer joy of having him in her arms, multiplied the pleasure streaking through her by a factor of ten. Twenty. A thousand.

They rolled together across the bed, legs tangled, mouths greedy, and Gillian stopping thinking altogether. She couldn't get enough of him. The taste of him. The sight of his face tight with desire. The feel of his smooth, taut muscles.

She was panting when he tore himself away and fished a condom out of his wallet, wet and eager when he kneed her legs apart. With a gasp of pure pleasure, she welcomed him into her heat.

The first time was hard and fast. The second time, so slow and incredible that Gillian discovered pleasure points she never knew she had.

The third time was just before dawn. Rain was still coming down with a steady patter when she woke. She lay quiet, enjoying the sound and the heavy weight of Hawk's arm draped across her waist.

Enjoyment soon gave way to a more pressing need. The rain reminded her she had to pee, like really bad. The longer she listened to the pinging drops, the worse she had to go. Finally she slithered out from under Hawk's arm and tiptoed to the bathroom.

As long as she was there, she might as well remove the night's fuzz from her teeth along with the sticky residue left over from their lovemaking. With both the bathroom door and the door to the shower shut tight, she figured she wouldn't disturb Hawk.

She figured wrong. She'd just worked up a nice lather when the shower door opened and Hawk muscled his way in. Dark bristles sprouted on his cheeks and chin. His hair looked as though he'd combed it with his fingers. His smile was slow and lazy and raised instant goose bumps on Gillian's naked skin.

"'Morning, Jade."

"Well, Hallelujah! I've finally made the transition." She flicked the washcloth at him. "And all it took was one night of wild sex."

He planted his palms against the tiles and caged her in. "The night's not officially over yet."

Hawk was dressed in jeans and had the international news on the flat-screen TV in the living room when Gillian emerged from the bedroom. She'd opted for casual, too. Gray slacks and a turtleneck sweater in bright, cheerful gold to combat the rain that had morphed into a torrential downpour, sheeting the windows and obscuring the cityscape outside.

"You ordered tea! Thank God!"

She made a beeline for the silver tray room service had delivered. While she'd downed a life-restoring infusion of Celestial Blossom, Hawk drummed his fingers against the table.

"I need to tell you about the DNA I took to the airport yesterday."

"Oh, Lord!" Disgusted, she shook her head. "I can't believe I let little things like a kidnapping, a long session with the Hong Kong police, dinner with the kids and three of the most explosive orgasms of my life make me forget that."

His grin slipped out. "That good, huh?"

"That good. So what's with the DNA? Whose is it?"

The grin faded. His face took on a grim cast that put a sudden damper on Gillian's lighthearted mood.

"I'm not sure," he said slowly. "I got the sample from Adriana but…"

He hesitated for several moments, prompting another question.

"Just out of curiosity, when and how did you obtain a sample of Hall's DNA?"

"Yesterday, after you came back to the hotel and Adriana and I went to the bank. She said McQuade had messengered over the documentation for the cloisonné pieces but she'd forgotten them. We went to her place to pick them up."

Stay cool, Gillian lectured sternly. Keep listening. No

need to get all itchy because Hawk made a little side trip with the Queen of Snide.

"While we were there, Adriana offered me a drink."

"Ha! I bet that's not all she offered."

The comment spilled out before she could stop it. Hawk shrugged but didn't deny the very real possibility Adriana had crawled all over him.

"When I said it was too early for a drink," he related slowly, "she tossed out the title of an old Alan Jackson–Jimmy Buffet song, 'It's Five O'clock Somewhere.'"

So Adriana liked country music? Unusual for the widow of a British lord, maybe, but the song was a classic. Gillian couldn't grasp the significance of the quote. The fact that Hawk went to stand in front of the windows, however, told her there was more to come.

It was a while coming. He stared unseeing into the rain pelting against the glass so long Gillian felt the lazy satisfaction left over from their session in the shower give way to a slow, tingling tension.

"Diane used to throw that line out, too," Hawk said at last.

"Who?"

He turned to face her. His expression was as neutral and as impenetrable as the fog shrouding the harbor.

"Diane Carr. She was an agent with the Drug Enforcement Agency."

Certainty burst inside Gillian, sucking the breath from her lungs. "The woman you once loved," she whispered.

"The woman I thought I loved."

His eyes held hers. She braced herself, not quite sure

she'd heard him correctly over the news coming through the speakers of the plasma TV.

"I realized yesterday I didn't have a clue what love was until you wormed your way into my heart."

Her breath whooshed out again. With the distinct sense that her world had just turned upside down, Gillian shoved away from the table and joined him at the windows.

"That wasn't the most romantic declaration I've ever received," she said on a shaky laugh, "but it will do. It will do very nicely. Now, please," she begged, "tell me what Adriana Hall has to do with a DEA agent named Diane Carr."

"I think…" A muscle ticked in one side of his jaw. "I think they may be the same woman."

Gillian's jaw dropped. She'd been imagining all sorts of wild possibilities. Maybe Carr had met Hall during an overseas posting. Maybe they'd become friends. Drinking buddies who crooned the same song while tossing back tequila shooters. That they might be one and the same had never even entered the realm of possibility!

"But I heard… Someone told me…" She gulped back her confusion and incomprehension. "Didn't the woman you knew as Diane Carr die?"

His eyes were bleak, his mind a thousand miles away. Her heart aching, Gillian laid a hand on his arm.

"Tell me," she said softly.

She didn't think he'd heard her. He was back in the jungle, reliving the horror.

"She took a bullet in the throat," he said at last. "I heard her choking. I tried to get to her."

The newscaster droned on in the background. His measured tones formed a counterpoint to Hawk's stark tale.

"They were still firing at us. The rounds sliced through vines, plowed into tree trunks. I took a couple of hits, too, and Charlie called in a chopper."

"Charlie?"

"Charlie Duncan. He was Special Ops then, like me."

"Wait a minute. Are you saying the agent who got his throat cut in San Francisco was there in the jungle with you and…and Diane?"

"Diane, or, as she might be going by now, Adriana."

"Good Lord!"

The implications were so staggering that Gillian couldn't process them. Her mind whirled as Hawk continued grimly.

"I went back for her after the docs dug out the bullets. I searched for weeks. I couldn't find her body or any villager who knew where it had been taken."

He stared at the sheets of rain, his shoulders rigid.

"I went back again, almost a year later. A rumor had surfaced that a gringo woman was living in the remote mountaintop stronghold of a drug lord. I led the raid that blasted into his lair, but he and his mistress escaped through a tunnel. The description of the woman given by others captured in the raid killed any hope she could be Diane."

He turned to face her then, and Gillian ached at the anguish in his face.

"I can still see her lying in that pool of blood. Still hear her choking. I couldn't save her, Jilly. I couldn't shield her."

"As you want to shield me," she murmured, heart-sick. She understood now why Hawk was so opposed to her joining OMEGA's ranks. She knew, too, that he would throw himself in front of a bullet to save her, as he tried to save the woman who might or might not be Adriana Hall.

If she *was* Diane, who would he choose?

The thought leaped into Gillian's head and stuck there, raising a host of sudden doubts.

If Adriana was the woman he'd once loved…

If she'd somehow survived…

If she'd been playing with Hawk all this time, stirring his memories, testing his bonds to his supposed wife…

Her stomach churning, Gillian tried to sort through her chaotic thoughts. The newscaster blathering on in the background didn't help. With a smothered curse, she snatched up the remote and aimed it at the big-screen TV. The next moment she went rigid with shock.

"Oh, my God!"

Hawk spun around. Horrified, Gillian pointed to the TV. "Look!"

The TV camera panned across the rows of shanties above the Mid-levels. With terrifying clarity, it zoomed in just as a solid wall of mud and debris began to slowly, inexorably slide down from above.

Chapter 14

Gillian and Hawk leaped out of the car that had whisked them through the high-speed tunnel and dropped them off as close as it could get to Hong Kong's outdoor escalator. Hawk had yanked on a jacket over his jeans, and Gillian had snatched up a raincoat to cover her slacks and sweater, but the rain hammered right through the plastic-coated fabric as she ran the remaining block and a half to the base station.

The scene that greeted them only compounded the fear that had clogged Gillian's throat since she and Hawk had watched the wall of mud descend on the shanties. Officials had reversed the escalator's direction to bring down dazed, mud-covered survivors. Frantic friends and relatives jammed the area, searching for their loved ones. Several banks and businesses near the base station had opened their doors to relief agencies for temporary shelters and processing centers.

"You check that shelter," Hawk shouted above the pounding rain. "I'll take this one."

Gillian darted up the steps and through the tall marble pillars of the Bank of China. A hundred or more bedraggled people huddled under blankets, sipping hot tea or soup.

Gillian scanned faces and feet, searching desperately for a pair of pink sneakers. Her hopes crashing, she spotted a woman with a clipboard.

"I'm looking for a boy about nine years old and a four-year-old girl," she told the relief worker. "Their names are Young Tau and Mei Lin. They'd be with an older gentleman named Ah Chang."

The woman flipped through her list. "We don't have them here, but we've set up three more shelters. There's another here at the base station, and two at the Mid-levels. You shouldn't try to get up there, though," she called as Gillian whirled. "It's a long climb. They'll be bringing people down when they can."

When she rushed out of the bank, the rain pelted her face. She blinked it out of her eyes and ran to the shelter Hawk had dashed into. She found him trying to communicate with a harried official and using hand gestures to indicate he was looking for a little girl, a taller boy and a stooped old man. Hope flared in his eyes when he spotted Gillian and died when she shook her head. In swift Cantonese, she queried the official.

"They're not here," she told Hawk, "but they've opened two more shelters at the Mid-levels."

"Let's go."

She didn't bother to repeat the first official's warning about the long climb. Hawk wouldn't heed it any more than she intended to.

The stair-stepping walkways on either side of the elevator were jammed with people surging upward while the moving stairs carried mud-covered evacuees downward. Some were sobbing, some clutched the few possessions they'd managed to save. Others were hollow-eyed with shock and disbelief. Gillian tried to search every face as she and Hawk jostled their way up level after level.

She had a stitch in her side by the tenth level and was gasping for breath by the thirteenth. Hawk practically dragged her to the sixteenth level. Forging a path through the throng, he came up against a set of sawhorse barriers and stopped dead.

"Oh, God!"

His low mutter stabbed into Gillian's heart. Flipping her wet hair out of her eyes, she blinked to clear her vision and felt her fear morph instantly into shock.

Half the hillside seemed to have given way and cut a huge brown swath through the tin-roofed shanties. Those directly in the onslaught's path had disappeared. The shanties on either side of the churned earth looked in imminent danger of going, as well. Some tipped precariously on their support poles. Others had completely collapsed. Fires, no doubt caused by overturned cooking braziers, had broken out in several places, hissing and spitting in the rain.

Rescue workers were frantically clearing everyone

out. Another section of the hillside could come roaring down at any moment, Gillian realized. Sick with fear, she searched the faces of the evacuees being led toward the barriers.

Suddenly, Hawk went stiff. "I recognize those two!"

He pointed to a young girl gripping the hand of a toddler in a quilted jacket and overalls with the seat cut out.

"Last time I saw them, the girl was holding him over a ditch to do his business. Ask her if she knows what happened to Young Tau or Mei Lin or Honorable Grandfather."

Gillian intercepted the pair and hunkered down. She sprang up a moment later with terror in her heart.

"She says she saw Young Tau and Mei Lin! They were trying to dig out Honorable Grandfather."

Cursing, Hawk leaped over the barriers. Gillian ignored the shouts of the official who tried to stop him and scuttled under.

They had to dodge evacuees and rescue workers and scattered debris. Rain and smoke obscured their vision. Twice they took a wrong turn in the maze of shanties and had to double back. Gillian had almost given up hope of finding the narrow opening that led to Ah Chang's place when Hawk spotted it.

"Here! Up here!"

He went first, ducking under tin roofs so close they almost touched. Gillian scrambled after him. When she cleared the narrow passageway, her heart dropped to her boots.

They stood at the very edge of the slide. Just a few feet ahead was a solid river of mud. Here, on the rim of that monstrous swath, houses tipped at crazy angles. So did the wooden steps leading up to Ah Chang's shanty.

"Hawk! Look! There's Mei Lin!"

They could just see the girl. She huddled at the top of the stairs, clutching a wooden cage and looking scared to death.

"Mei Lin!" Hawk shouted. "Mei Lin!"

Her head whipped up. A high, thin wail carried through the rain. "Cal-Han *Shen Sheung!*"

"We're coming," Gillian shouted, scrambling after Hawk. "Don't move, baby. Don't move."

The stairs tilted even more under Hawk's weight and for a terrified moment Gillian was sure they'd give. To her infinite relief, they made it to the top. Hawk scooped up a sobbing Mei Lin and her drenched canary. Two seconds later, he shoved them both into Gillian's arms and raced to aid Young Tau. Panting, sobbing, straining, the boy was struggling to lift the corrugated tin roof that had collapsed and opened the shanty's front room to the rain.

Hawk grabbed an edge and heaved. An ominous creak sounded from the support poles dug into the hillside beneath his feet, but the tin lifted with a loud ponging sound. Young Tau dropped to all fours and crawled inside. His panicked shout echoed out a moment later.

"Back of roof fell in, blocks Honorable Grandfather. He can't get out."

Gillian plunked Mei Lin down and propped a shoulder under the corrugated tin. "I'll hold it."

"It's too heavy for you."

"I'll hold it! Get Ah Chang."

Every moment it took to free Ah Chang felt like a thousand. Gillian refused to think about the rain slamming down or the mountain of dirt still waiting to break loose.

Young Tau scrambled out first. Hawk backed out next, his arms hooked under the old man's armpits. As soon as Ah Chang was clear of the tin, Hawk slung him up into his arms.

"Let's get the hell out of Dodge!"

They had just made it to the barriers when an ominous rumble sounded behind them. Gillian threw a look over her shoulder and felt her heart stop when the hillside above Ah Chang's shanty seemed to implode. Tons of soaked earth broke loose. Seconds later, what was left of the dwelling was buried under an avalanche of mud.

The Peninsula's doormen were too well trained to gawk, but they came close when a taxi disgorged five soaked and muddy passengers several hours later.

Gillian and Hawk had insisted on taking Honorable Grandfather to the emergency room to have him checked over. The ER doc confirmed Ah Chang's self-diagnosis that he was shaken but not hurt.

All of them were shaken. Mei Lin wouldn't let Hawk put her down. She clung to him like a burr, one arm locked around his neck. With her other, she kept a death grip on the cage containing her bedraggled canary. Young Tau tried his best to hold back his tears when he'd discovered he'd lost his iPod, but he climbed out of the cab with twin streaks down his dirty cheeks. Gillian's stomach knotted every time she thought about how close all of them had come to being buried alive.

They left a trail of muddy footprints through the Peninsula's pristine lobby. As soon as they got to the suite, Gillian pried a protesting Mei Lin out of Hawk's arms.

"It's okay, baby. We'll just wash off the mud. Yes, we'll get your birdie clean, too."

She hiked the girl higher and switched to English.

"I'll take her into the master bath. Hawk, show Young Tau and Honorable Grandfather the other bathroom. Then call down to the gift shop. Tell them to send up some clothing suitable for a four-year-old girl, a ten-year-old boy and an elderly Chinese gentleman ASAP."

Hawk made the call while Honorable Grandfather soaked in a steaming tub and Young Tau scrubbed off in the shower. With Ah Chang wrapped in one of the Peninsula's robes and the kid encased in a supersize bath towel, Hawk took his turn in the shower.

He made it quick. He knew Gillian was still pretty shook up. So were the kids. Hell, it would take *him* a long time to forget the sucking, sickening sound of a whole damned hillside coming loose.

He left his filthy clothes in a heap with Young Tau's and Ah Chang's and pulled a pair of khakis and a white shirt out of the closet. Once dressed, force of habit had him closing and locking the bedroom door so he could clean the weapon that had nested at the small of his back. He started to clip the holster onto his belt and hesitated. Better not, while the kids were here. The Glock went into the room safe alongside Gillian's Beretta.

When he strolled into the living room, a now-yellow canary was perched atop one of the porcelain ginger jars and tissue paper littered every square inch of the floor.

Gillian saw him take in the scene with a raised brow. She'd warn him later, when they were alone, that this was nothing compared to the purchases they'd have to make to help Ah Chang and the kids get back on their feet.

"You did good," she told him as a scrubbed and blow-dried Mei Lin paraded around the room in a long-sleeved yellow T-shirt trimmed with lace daisies, matching overalls and frilly socks. The shiny, white patent leather Mary Janes were too big for her tiny feet, but she absolutely refused to part with them.

Young Tau was still desolate over the loss of his iPod. Not even designer jeans and a polo shirt sporting the Peninsula's distinctive logo could console him. Ah Chang's brocaded silk robe trailed the floor a little due to his stoop, but the length wasn't his concern. His expression troubled, he fingered the rich silk.

"This is too fine for such an old man, Jill-An."

"You look very distinguished in it, Honorable Grandfather."

"I cannot accept such a gift. It is too expensive."

"It isn't a gift. We have an agreement, remember? Cal-Han and I owe you a commission for checking out our purchases."

She swept a hand toward the tall cloisonné candlesticks still holding a place of honor on the coffee table.

"The commission on those pieces alone will replace much of what you lost today."

His cloudy eyes looked from her to Hawk. Behind the old man's back, Gillian bobbed her head up and down in a vigorous motion. Hawk got the message and nodded.

With a small smile, Ah Chang turned back to Gillian. "Cal-Han understands not a word, does he?"

"No, Honorable Grandfather."

"Yet he agrees with what you say."

"Occasionally."

"You have a good man, Jill-An."

Some of the horror of the morning lifted.

"Yes," Gillian replied softly, "I do."

Hawk felt his watch begin to vibrate while everyone was feasting on a lunch of hot and sour soup, shrimp-stuffed dumplings and noodles steamed with cabbage and carrots. Excusing himself, he went into the bedroom and closed the door. Griff came on as soon as Hawk acknowledged the transmission.

"We just got the results. The DNA is a match."

Hawk stood rigid, every muscle taut, every tendon corded. The elegance of the master bedroom faded. The murmur of voices in the other room died. The rain splatting against the windows grew louder, sharper, like sniper bullets slicing through tangled vines.

"Hawk? Did you read me?"

"I read you, Ace." The reply was automatic. Empty. "Thanks."

Griff signed off, and still Hawk didn't move. Every part of him felt frozen. His arms, his legs, his mind.

He had no idea how long he stood there. It might have been seconds, minutes, hours, before he heard a loud buzz.

The door. Someone was at the main door to the suite.

His mind was still shut down, but blind instinct kicked in. Automatically, his hand went to the small of his back. The empty hollow where his weapon usually nested jerked him back to reality.

Adriana. Diane. Charlie Duncan.

An icy coldness settled in the pit of his stomach. Kids or not, he had business to take care of. The coldness spread as he punched in the code for the hotel safe and clipped on his Glock. His navy blazer covered the holster as he strode out of the bedroom.

Ah Chang and the kids were still at the table, wielding chopsticks. Gillian stood in the foyer. Her face was dead white.

"We…" She swiped her tongue over her lower lip. "We have a visitor."

Hawk's gaze locked on the woman behind her. "So I see."

Diane. How could that be Diane? The hair, the face, the voice, even the eyes were different.

Those unfamiliar eyes fixed on Hawk and hardened to glittering green glass. "You know, don't you?"

"Yes."

She let out a long, slow hiss. Then casually, so casually, she angled around enough for Hawk to see the silencer a few inches from Gillian's back.

"I didn't plan to do it here," she said with chilling nonchalance, "but the fools I hired to snatch your 'wife' and lure you to a more isolated locale bungled the job." Without shifting her gaze, she nodded to the trio at the table. "Get rid of them."

"They don't have anywhere to go," Gillian protested. "They lost everything in the mud slide and…"

She broke off, wincing as the silencer dug into her ribs.

"Get rid of them, Callahan."

"They've seen you." Hawk knew it was useless to point out the obvious but had to try. "They can describe you to the police."

"They'll describe a woman who won't exist after today." Her husky voice took on a raw edge. "Just like Diane Carr ceased to exist. She died in that stinking jungle where you and Charlie left her."

The hate spilled out, low and savage.

"Get rid of them, Callahan, unless you want them to witness what happens next. And keep your hands where I can see them! I've been waiting a long time for this moment. I don't want it to end too soon."

"Young Tau."

The boy looked up from his dumplings.

"Do me a favor, kid. Take Honorable Grandfather and Mei Lin down to the lobby."

"We still eat."

"I know. But you're almost finished. There's a bakery just off the lobby. Order any dessert you want, and tell them to charge it to our room."

"But…"

"Jill-An and I have business to conduct with this woman. Honorable Grandfather will understand."

Frowning, Young Tau laid down his chopsticks and translated the request. Ah Chang acceded with a nod. Mei Lin pursed her lips and countered with a request of her own.

"Little sister asks if she can leave canary."

"Yeah, sure."

As the three rose from the table, Diane nudged

Gillian out of the foyer and into the living room. They might have been two friends strolling side by side to admire the cloisonné candlesticks on the coffee table.

"Have one of the clerks at the desk call the room before you come up," Hawk told Young Tau, fighting to sound natural. Everything inside him cringed at the possibility the kids might return and get caught in a cross fire. "Our business may take a while."

A stark silence blanketed the suite after the door closed. Diane broke it by moving far enough across the room to give her an angle on both Gillian and Hawk. Her smile sliced into his heart.

"Charlie didn't recognize me. Not even when I had the knife to his throat. How'd you break the code, Callahan?"

"The perfume. The SIG Sauer P226. The title of that old song."

"What song?"

"'It's Five O'clock Somewhere.'"

"Hell! When did that slip out?"

"Yesterday, at your condo. Right before I knocked our glasses off the table."

Comprehension twisted her perfect features into an ugly mask. "Sunnuvabitch! You took one of those glass shards, didn't you?"

Hawk nodded. He wanted her looking in his direction, wanted her attention focused solely on him. When he made his move, Gillian would be out of the line of fire.

"Yes, I took one of the shards. And I just got word a few minutes ago the DNA was a match. They know you're alive, Diane. They'll…"

"Diane's dead!" she lashed back. "She died when you abandoned her."

The wounds had opened up. Hers. His. Hawk felt them bleed as she spewed out her rage and pain.

"The woman who survived against all odds... The woman who spread her legs for the bastard who raped and beat her to a bloody pulp for the sheer sport of it... The woman who finally killed the pig and stole his blood money... That's the woman who derived immense satisfaction from slitting Charlie Duncan's throat."

Her eyes glittered. The gun in her hand never wavered.

"I knew you'd pick up where Charlie left off and follow the leads I planted so carefully. I knew you'd want to avenge his death, although you made no effort to avenge mine."

"That's not true!"

Gillian's protest knifed across the room.

"Hawk went back for you. As soon as his wounds healed. He told me he searched for weeks. And again, a year later. He led a raid on some drug lord's mountaintop stronghold where a gringo woman was supposedly living."

The blonde's gaze whipped to Hawk. "That was you?"

For a moment, just a moment, Gillian was sure she saw regret and something that looked like despair flicker across the other woman's face.

"You were too late, Mike. By then, I'd become what they'd made me. The only thing that kept me alive was plotting and planning ways to make you and Charlie suffer as much as I did. And you handed me the perfect opportunity."

There wasn't a trace of regret in either her face or her voice now.

"You're going to watch her wallow in her own blood, Callahan. You're going to listen to her crying and moaning and sobbing your name. Then you'll die, too."

"It's not going down that way, Diane. You know it. I know it."

Gillian sensed Hawk coiling, knew he'd lunge and draw the bullet intended for her. So did the blond bitch across from them. Her aim shifted.

"Don't do it, Callahan."

With the other woman's entire being focused on Hawk, Gillian knew this was the only chance she'd get.

She didn't stop to think. Didn't calculate her chances. Acting on blind instinct, she wrapped a hand around one of the heavy candlesticks and swung it in a vicious arc.

The blonde caught the movement and ducked. Gillian didn't hear the silenced shots, only a thud as a bullet plowed into the wall behind her and the crack of a window shattering. She heard Hawk's Glock, though.

The gun flew out of the blonde's hand. She gave a cry of pain and cradled her arm.

Gillian thought it was over. She was sure it was done. Trembling all over, she sucked in a breath that carried the stink of cordite.

The flash of naked steel took her completely by surprise. She saw the blonde's other arm come up, caught a glimpse of the serrated blade, heard Hawk shout a warning.

"Don't do it, Diane!"

"It's me or her, Callahan. Make your choice. One of us is going to die."

Her arm whipped forward.

Hawk's Glock bucked in his hand.

Epilogue

The van OMEGA had sent to the airport at Hawk's request pulled into the circular drive of the Ridgeways' two-story brick residence. October winds had stripped the leaves from the maples and oaks, but the clay pots filled with white geraniums decorated the brick front steps and offered a warm welcome.

Hawk got out of the van first and went back to lift out Mei Lin and her canary. Transporting the damned bird to the States had cost him hours of paperwork and a hefty sum in bribes. Same with the temporary visas for Ah Chang and the kids. Gillian had used her pull at the U.S. Embassy, but Hawk had to grease a few palms before Chinese officials issued the necessary documentation.

Young Tau climbed out of the van next, sprouting a

new set of ear buds, while Gillian assisted Ah Chang. She'd called ahead, so the entire Ridgeway clan had been on the lookout. Including Tank, she'd learned, who was on a fall break from Harvard.

"Brace yourself," she warned in Cantonese. "My family is very large and very noisy."

Even with the warning, the chaos that erupted when her mother threw open the front door startled a small shriek from Mei Lin.

"Ai-ah!"

Radizwell raced out first, prancing and barking his fool head off. He was followed in short order by Gillian's sister, Samantha, her parents and Tank. Her jaw dropped when she spotted the tiny ape perched on her brother's shoulder.

"Radizwell! Down! Quiet!"

Gillian's exasperated commands finally penetrated the sheepdog's joy at seeing her again. She returned her mother's fierce hug, but before she made the necessary introductions, she had to ask.

"Where did Tank get the furry neckpiece?"

"Your friend Ben Nareesh dropped him off two days ago. He said you told him to claim the creature if and when it cleared quarantine."

"That isn't exactly what I told him. Er, how does Terrence the Lizard get along with the monkey?"

"He doesn't," her father drawled. "Good to see you, Hawk. We heard what happened in Hong Kong. That was some damned fine shooting."

Gillian didn't want to relive that awful instant when Hawk's shot shattered the knife in midflight. The pieces rained down at the same instant Gillian swung the cloi-sonné candlestick again.

She connected the second time. Adriana Hall…Diane Carr…now sat in a Hong Kong prison awaiting extradition to the U.S. And, she thought with a spark of happiness that warmed her from the inside out, Hawk had finally buried his past.

"Mom, Dad, this is Ah Chang." Smoothly, she switched to Chinese. "Honorable Grandfather, these are my parents."

Adam returned Ah Chang's bow. "Please tell him we're honored to welcome him to our home."

Tank joined them then. The gibbon had crawled up his neck and was now wrapped around his head like a turban. Mei Lin gaped at the two of them from the safety of Hawk's arms, but Tank gained an instant pal in Young Tau when he pulled his iPod out of his jeans pocket.

"Do you like the Red Bananas?"

The boy's eyes rounded. "You have songs by Red Bananas?"

"Every CD they've put out. C'mon, you can plug into my computer and download the songs onto your iPod."

Gillian could have kissed him when he looped an arm around the boy's shoulders. Her little brother was now six-two and as broad-shouldered as their dad but a lot more laid-back.

"And who's this sweetheart?" Gillian's sister cooed.

"This is Mei Lin."

"Hi, Mei Lin. I'm Samantha."

"She's a little unnerved by the long trip," Gillian warned. "She won't leave Hawk's arms."

"Sure she will."

Smiling, Sam produced the object she'd tucked under one arm. The stuffed tiger was missing an eye and had had his tail sewn back on twice, but his silly grin made an instant hit with Mei Lin. Transferring her canary to Hawk, she fell into Samantha's arms.

"Let's go inside," Maggie suggested, her maternal antennae quivering. Something had happened in Hong Kong, something Gillian hadn't included in her telephone report to her family. She had a glow about her, and the smile she gave Hawk when they started up the walk was *not* the kind one field operative gave another.

She contained her impatience until the adults had gathered in the den. Adam poured Ah Chang a glass of restorative brandy and offered one to Hawk.

"I'll have one, too," Gillian said. "Mom, too. I want to make a toast."

Her father hooked a brow but dutifully splashed Courvoisier into Waterford snifters and passed them around. The brandy's aromatic fumes tickled Gillian's nose as she held up her glass.

"Here's to you," she said to her parents. "Thanks for putting us all up. We *had* to have Mei Lin, Young Tau and Honorable Grandfather at the wedding."

Her father's brows snapped together as she repeated the toast in Chinese for Ah Chang. By the time she'd finished, her mother wore a broad smile.

"I told her you'd be tough to bring down, Hawk. How did she manage it?"

"Damned if I know." With a wry grin, his arm slid around Gillian's waist. "I think it was *feng shui.*"

His grin faded as he stared down at the woman who'd turned his world upside down and, with the swing of a candlestick, had made it right again.

"Wind and water," he murmured. "Darkness and light. Male and female."

Laughter danced in her blue eyes. "You're mixing *feng shui* with yin and yang. Better get the concepts straight before we go back to Hong Kong for our honeymoon. The real one, this time."

The interested observers forgotten, Hawk tightened his hold. "I may have the concepts confused, but I know this much, Gillian-with-a-J. Whatever happens with the kids and Honorable Grandfather, however we decide to work our jobs with OMEGA, you restored balance and harmony in my life."

Harmony was good. Love was better.

Gillian saw it in his face and felt the joy of it in every corner of her heart.

"Think we can we throw together a wedding by this weekend, Mom?"

"Consider it done."

* * * * *

Here's a sneak peek at
THE CEO'S CHRISTMAS PROPOSITION,
the first in USA TODAY *bestselling author*
Merline Lovelace's
HOLIDAYS ABROAD *trilogy*
coming in November 2008.

American Devon McShay is about to get the Christmas surprise of a lifetime when she meets her new client, sexy billionaire Caleb Logan, for the very first time.

Silhouette
Desire

Available November 2008

Her breath whistled out in a sigh of relief when he exited Customs. Devon recognized him right away from the newspaper and magazine articles her friend and partner Sabrina had looked up during her frantic prep work.

Caleb John Logan, Jr. Thirty-one. Six-two. With jet-black hair, laser-blue eyes and a linebacker's shoulders under his charcoal-gray cashmere overcoat. His jaw-dropping good looks didn't score him any points with Devon. She'd learned the hard way not to trust handsome heartbreakers like Cal Logan.

But he was a client. An important one. And she was willing to give someone who'd served a hitch in the marines before earning a B.S. from the University of Oregon, an MBA from Stanford and his first million at the ripe old age of twenty-six the benefit of the doubt.

Right up until he spotted the hot-pink pashmina, that is.

Devon knew the flash of color was more visible than the sign she held up with his name on it. So she wasn't surprised when Logan picked her out of the crowd and cut in her direction. She'd just plastered on her best businesswoman smile when he whipped an arm around her waist. The next moment she was sprawled against his cashmere-covered chest.

"Hello, brown eyes."

Swooping down, he covered her mouth with his.

Sheer astonishment kept Devon rooted to the spot for a few seconds while her mind whirled chaotically. Her first thought was that her client had downed a few too many drinks during the long flight. Her second, that he'd mistaken the kind of escort and consulting services her company provided. Her third shoved everything else out of her head.

The man could kiss!

His mouth moved over hers with a skill that ignited sparks at a half dozen flash points throughout her body. Devon hadn't experienced that kind of spontaneous combustion in a while. A *long* while.

The sparks were still popping when she pushed off his chest, only now they fueled a flush of anger.

"Do you always greet women you don't know with a lip-lock, Mr. Logan?"

A smile crinkled the skin at the corners of his eyes. "As a matter of fact, I don't. That was from Don."

"Huh?"

"He said he owed you one from New Year's Eve two years ago and made me promise to deliver it."

She stared up at him in total incomprehension. Logan hooked a brow and attempted to prompt a non-existent memory.

"He abandoned you at the Waldorf. Five minutes before midnight. To deliver twins."

"I don't have a clue who or what you're..."

Understanding burst like a water balloon.

"Wait a sec. Are you talking about Sabrina's old boy-friend? Your buddy, who's now an ob-gyn doc?"

It was Logan's turn to look startled. He recovered faster than Devon had, though. His smile widened into a rueful grin.

"I take it you're not Sabrina Russo."

"No, Mr. Logan, I am *not*."

* * * * *

Be sure to look for
THE CEO'S CHRISTMAS PROPOSITION
by Merline Lovelace.
Available in November 2008 wherever books are sold,
including most bookstores, supermarkets, drugstores
and discount stores.

REQUEST YOUR FREE BOOKS!

2 FREE NOVELS PLUS 2 FREE GIFTS!

Silhouette® Romantic

SUSPENSE

Sparked by Danger, Fueled by Passion!

YES! Please send me 2 FREE Silhouette® Romantic Suspense novels and my 2 FREE gifts (gifts are worth about $10). After receiving them, if I don't wish to receive any more books, I can return the shipping statement marked "cancel." If I don't cancel, I will receive 4 brand-new novels every month and be billed just $4.24 per book in the U.S. or $4.99 per book in Canada, plus 25¢ shipping and handling per book plus applicable taxes, if any*. That's a savings of at least 15% off the cover price! I understand that accepting the 2 free books and gifts places me under no obligation to buy anything. I can always return a shipment and cancel at any time. Even if I never buy another book from Silhouette, the two free books and gifts are mine to keep forever.

240 SDN EEX6 340 SDN EEYJ

Name	(PLEASE PRINT)	
Address		Apt. #
City	State/Prov.	Zip/Postal Code

Signature (if under 18, a parent or guardian must sign)

Mail to the **Silhouette Reader Service:**
IN U.S.A.: P.O. Box 1867, Buffalo, NY 14240-1867
IN CANADA: P.O. Box 609, Fort Erie, Ontario L2A 5X3

Not valid to current subscribers of Silhouette Romantic Suspense books.

Want to try two free books from another line?
Call 1-800-873-8635 or visit www.morefreebooks.com.

* Terms and prices subject to change without notice. N.Y. residents add applicable sales tax. Canadian residents will be charged applicable provincial taxes and GST. Offer not valid in Quebec. This offer is limited to one order per household. All orders subject to approval. Credit or debit balances in a customer's account(s) may be offset by any other outstanding balance owed by or to the customer. Please allow 4 to 6 weeks for delivery. Offer available while quantities last.

Your Privacy: Silhouette is committed to protecting your privacy. Our Privacy Policy is available online at www.eHarlequin.com or upon request from the Reader Service. From time to time we make our lists of customers available to reputable third parties who may have a product or service of interest to you. If you would prefer we not share your name and address, please check here. ☐

SRS08R

Romantic
SUSPENSE

**Sparked by Danger,
Fueled by Passion.**

Lindsay McKenna
Susan Grant

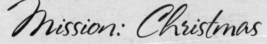

Celebrate the holidays with a pair
of military heroines and their daring men
in two romantic, adventurous stories
from these bestselling authors.

Featuring:

"The Christmas Wild Bunch"
by *USA TODAY* bestselling author
Lindsay McKenna

and

"Snowbound with a Prince"
by *New York Times* bestselling author
Susan Grant

Available November wherever books are sold.

Inside ROMANCE

Stay up-to-date on all your romance reading news!

The Inside Romance newsletter is a FREE quarterly newsletter highlighting our upcoming series releases and promotions!

Click on the <u>Inside Romance</u> link on the front page of
www.eHarlequin.com or e-mail us at
insideromance@harlequin.ca to sign up
to receive your FREE newsletter today!

You can also subscribe by writing us at: HARLEQUIN BOOKS
Attention: Customer Service Department
P.O. Box 9057, Buffalo, NY 14269-9057

Please allow 4-6 weeks for delivery of the first issue by mail.

Silhouette® Romantic SUSPENSE

COMING NEXT MONTH

#1535 MISSION: CHRISTMAS
"The Christmas Wild Bunch" by Lindsay McKenna
"Snowbound with a Prince" by Susan Grant
Celebrate the holidays with a pair of military heroines and their daring men in two romantic, adventurous short stories from these bestselling authors.

#1536 THE SHERIFF'S AMNESIAC BRIDE—Linda Conrad
The Coltons: Family First
When a woman on the run shows up in his life, Sheriff Jericho Yates takes her in. The trouble is—she can't remember who she is or why someone was shooting at her! As "Rosie" and Jericho uncover bits about her past, they must dodge the goons who are after her, all while trying to ignore their undeniable attraction.

#1537 MANHUNTER—Loreth Anne White
Wild Country
Isolated in the Yukon with 24-hour nights and endless snow, Mountie Gabriel Caruso is forced to team up with Silver Karvonen, a local tracker, to hunt down a sadistic serial killer bent on revenge. While the murderer plays mind games with them, Gabe and Silver face their biggest fears while growing ever closer…one footprint at a time.

#1538 TO PROTECT A PRINCESS—Gail Barrett
The Crusaders
When Roma princess Dara Adams teams up with reluctant mountain guide Logan Burke to find a lost artifact, their lives—and their hearts—are on the line. But they're not the only ones searching for the treasure, and danger lurks around every corner. Harboring secrets that could change everything, Dara and Logan battle their desire for each other while fighting for their lives.